The Undead Stars

Jacqueline Elisabeth

For anyone that needs music to survive

Chapter One

The theater lights go down and the five of us step out onto the stage. The crowd bursts into cheers as we take our spots. I close my eyes for a second and position my hands on my guitar as I hear our super sexy drummer, Finnley Emmerson, count us in. I look to them for a second, sitting at the drums in a simple black tank top with their head down, a mop of curls hiding their face.

"Kyle, I love you!" someone screams from the crowd. Though I can't see who it is, I can't help but blush. I've seen the comments all over our social media, I've somehow become the fan favorite, or the heartthrob, whichever term you'd prefer. They both feel weird to me. I'm just the guy who plays guitar, nothing more and nothing less. It's who I am. But as my cousin Perri loves to say, the ginger hair and goofy smile seem to do something for the girls.

I turn back to the crowd as the stage lights come up and we start to play the intro we spent weeks perfecting for this tour. I start to search the crowd, looking for my parents and not finding them. Why would I even think they would come to the opening show of my band's summer tour? I'm never anything more than the disappointment who won't follow in my father's footsteps. No matter what I do, it's never enough. And now he's not here. But it's not related. If I ask him about it later, he'll say something about work. I'm sure he's got a great excuse.

I scan the crowd, finding my cousin and her girlfriend standing towards the front, having the time of their lives and then, at the very back of the venue, my parents. My mom looks happy, almost. My father, however, looks like he'd rather be anywhere else.

As our intro comes to an end I focus on our first song as we bleed right into it. My fingers find the chords naturally as we start to play. I relax more as I play, finding the fun in the music. I love this song. I *wrote* this song. It's one of my cousin's favorites.

As we head into the first chorus, I close my eyes and forget we're on stage. In my mind we're in the garage we always rehearse in. I imagine Finn at the old, beaten-up drum set with their head down, that one poster behind them. The one I never really understood, and then they look up and their eyes meet mine, and they smile, and everything feels just as it should.

I open my eyes, and I'm back on stage as we move into the second verse. Across the stage, one of my best friends and our bassist, Maristella Thompson, loving called Mari, jumps to the beat, the blue underside of her hair catches the lights as we vibe together through the second verse.

Once we transition into the next chorus, everything starts to feel right. The crowd is screaming and for the first time I realize that this is going to be my life for the next three months. For the next three months, we're going to be on tour doing this every single night.

The crowd is loud and electric and I'm truly feeding off of it. Since our band blew up about six months ago, we haven't truly had a moment where we got to experience seeing and being with our fans. If that's even what we should be calling them. It feels weird to say we have fans, but after taking off on social media and getting signed by a record label, this tour was the natural next step after the success of our EP

We transition into the bridge of the song and it's my favorite part. Mari, Finn, and I all cut back on what we're playing to allow Aspen Owens, the blonde cutie on the keys, to have her full moment. This part of the song is always so beautiful. It might be one of my favorite things I have ever written, if I can say that. The melodic keys against the sultry vocals at the start are so peaceful and then slowly the rest of us come back in giving the edge of the bridge that punch at the end. That normally pulls us right into the final chorus. But not this time.

We continue vamping on the chord progression and the tiny, yet feisty, brunette standing front and center calls into the microphone "Boston! How are you feeling tonight!" The crowd goes wild, and my fingers slip for the briefest of seconds. They're just so loud. Nothing could have prepared me for this. "If you've never seen our faces before, we are The Undead Stars!" The second time I'm more prepared for the screaming that comes from the audience. It's electrifying. They are here for *us*, and it shows. "Before we go ahead and finish this song, is it cool if I introduce the rest of my band?" As the crowd cheers once again, Mari looks to me and I can't help but burst out laughing. Luckily, I'm standing just far enough away from my microphone that it doesn't get picked up for the whole crowd to hear.

"Well to my left is probably one of the coolest people I know, if her blue hair didn't give that away, give it up for our incredible bassist Mari!" Mari dives into this really fun riff on the bass that has us all jumping.

"And that cute little blonde next to her on the keys is my best friend, Aspen!" Aspen blushes slightly as she plays the keyboard solo she's been practicing and perfecting for months. She has the biggest smile on her face when she finishes. She's so proud of herself and I love to see it.

"Now on the other side of me, we have everyone's favorite on guitar, Kyle!" She calls out and then it's my turn. I close my eyes as I play the guitar solo I've spent so much time practicing. Every single time I play it it's different. I feel it again as I play it, the subtle changes that I don't even realize I'm making. The way I slightly fumble the start due to nerves and the way I skip a small section towards the middle. But I finish gracefully and step back.

"Now, if you look at the very back of the stage, you can see that the mess of dark curls is actually our drummer, Finn!" I turn to look at Finn and that might have been a mistake. I almost stop playing as I watch them. They look up and smile for half a second before launching into their drum solo and I can't tear my eyes away. They throw their head back and close their eyes and I can't help but find something about the way they're playing to be almost sexual. And there I'm reminded of the crush I've had for years on the member of the band that I'm the closest with.

The only member of this band who happens to be in a relationship.

When they finish their drum solo, I swear they meet my stare and smile as they go back to what they were playing before.

"And I'm Harper! This is Chasing Shadows, we hope you enjoy!" We jump right back into the song, playing out the final chorus, and just like that the first song of the evening comes to an end.

♬

We come off the stage and the first thing I do is grab a water bottle, chugging half of it before sitting down on the couch backstage. I can't help but watch as Finn practically runs over to their girlfriend, our manager, and Mari's cousin, Stevie to give her a big sweaty hug and kiss. I wish that could have been me. There's a giant pizza waiting for us, and the girls immediately grab plates and start to dig in. I'm hungry. I want some. But there's something about watching Finn grabbing a slice with Stevie on their lap that makes me want to skip out on dinner. I grab three slices anyway.

"Someone's hungry," Mari says, eyeing my plate.

"Why are you acting so surprised? We all know he can eat." Finn teases, a smirk playing at their lips.

I stare down at my hands as I continue to eat, trying to focus on my chipped nail polish instead of Finn's comment.

"And how do you know so much about how much Kyle eats?" Mari asks Finn with a mischievous glint in her eyes. "Is there something you're not telling us?" With that comment Stevie looks up from her plate and shoots Finn a look I can't discern. But she doesn't look happy.

"All I'm saying is we've all seen the way Kyle can eat." Finn says quietly.

"So, you're paying attention to how much I'm eating?" I ask, liking the way their attention on me feels, and maybe a small part of me even likes the way that Stevie glowers.

"I'm just saying we eat a lot of meals together!" they try to defend themself.

"Right. That's all you're trying to say." I can't help but smile as I see the tiniest hint of a blush creep up their cheeks. I can feel Stevie's eyes on me, and I don't even have to look over to know that she looks pissed. I can see it on everyone else's faces.

"That felt really good!" Aspen says, trying to break through the very obvious tension in the room. She smiles awkwardly as we all kind of look at her but no one says anything.

Luckily, we're saved from the awkwardness when all of our friends and family who were at the show make their way backstage to congratulate us and celebrate the start of the tour.

"That was amazing!" my cousin Perri says as she runs over to me, nearly pouncing on me, with her girlfriend Aubrey following not far behind. I smile as she hugs me, watching as everyone's parents and friends start filing in and finding my own amongst the crowd. "It never ceases to amaze me that my cousin's a big famous rockstar now." Perri laughs, making room for my parents to come into the little circle we've found ourselves in.

"You were incredible tonight," Aubrey says softly as she hugs me. She glues herself to Perri's side as the small room is filled with more and more people, quickly getting loud and overwhelming.

"Are you excited to hit the road?" Perri asks, and I know she sees the way my father is standing off to the side of the group as if he's preparing to criticize everything about this.

"Yeah, I can't wait to see the country like this. I wish you could come with me though, both of you really," I say looking between my cousin and my best friend.

"You'll just have to text us every single day. Do you think you can do that?" I know Perri isn't trying to be condescending. I easily forget to check my texts, let alone reply, but I can't help but feel like that's a slight dig at me.

"I will do my best, I promise," I say with a smile as everyone around me falls into conversation with one another. Leaving my father the perfect opportunity to pull me aside, away from the group, to talk.

"So, uh, what did you think?" I ask him hoping I don't come across as the nervous mess I feel like the longer he looks at me.

"You were good," he says, his tone clipped as he looks off towards something behind me. I don't dare turn around to see what he's looking at.

"Thanks," I reply nervously, waiting for him to meet my eyes.

He doesn't say anything for a few minutes, and I wish someone could just swoop in and pull me away from him, give me something else to talk about or someone else to talk to. *Someone. Anyone. Please.*

"You painted your nails," he says eventually and I hold my breath as I nod, slowly looking down at the black nail polish on my fingers.

"I did, yeah." I don't want to look up at him and see the disappointment written all over his face. "Finn painted them actually," I say trying to fill the space. I watch as my father slowly turns his head to look in Finn's direction, nearly glaring, before directing his gaze back to me.

"I thought we talked about this." He brings his voice down to a whisper to make sure no one hears and I didn't think it was possible for me to shrink even more under his gaze, yet I do.

"I know, but that was in a professional setting. And I thought it looked cool. The black kind of matches my guitar. And with the rings..." I let my voice trail off as I flex the fingers of my right hand.

"You're a man, are you not?" I swear the room goes quiet when he says that, though it seems no one is actually paying attention to us. I feel it deep in my bones. I know no one in the room is looking at us, but I feel everyone's stare anyway. "Are you not?" my father asks again when I don't answer immediately.

"I am," I say as I spin a ring on my right pointer finger.

"That's what I thought. So why is it that a son of mine thinks it is okay for men to wear nail polish?"

I swallow thickly and look down at my hands again. "I just thought it looked cool, and plenty of male musicians do it."

His gaze narrows and I feel my breath start to pick up against my own will.

"That's the excuse you want to go with?"

My mom, sensing the tone of my father's voice comes over and gently puts a hand on his arm.

"I just like the way it looks." I say, feeling like I'm repeating myself, but it doesn't matter.

"I thought we've been over this," he hisses. "I'm going to have to be okay with this whole gay phase you're going through. I promised your mother that, but do you have to make it so visible? You don't need to go parading it around for everyone to see."

And there it was. The reason behind the outburst. How had I not seen it sooner? It's just another reminder that nothing I do will ever be good enough for him unless it's the path and the future *he* wants for me. I hate that moments like this make me consider quitting the band and going to college for business, getting a masters, and then living in my father's shadow. Being a carbon copy of him. Maybe that's all I'm destined to be.

"It's just nail polish," I say softly. I look down at my hands again and, without even realizing, I've spent most of our conversation picking off the nail polish that I had been wearing. "I'll take it off when we get to the hotel. I'm sure one of the girls has nail polish remover," I say eventually, hoping that it'll get him to calm down and drop it.

My dad nods and turns to my mother, making an excuse about having to be up early the next morning before heading out, dragging Perri and Aubrey with them since they all rode in together.

I look around the room for a minute, seeing everyone else happy with their friends and family, celebrating the show and the beginning of the tour. I can't help but feel jealous. The only person who doesn't seem to have anyone hanging out and celebrating is Stevie, and there is no way I can go over there.

I sit back down on the couch, distancing myself from everyone as Stevie sends us all the pictures that were taken during the show. I scroll through and they all look really good. We all look really good. But in each picture of me, I can't help but focus in on the nail polish. I should have known better than to wear nail polish like that. It's just so prominent. You can't not see it.

I pull a few photos into photoshop and start messing around with them, trying to get rid of the nail polish while keeping it looking natural. It's not working. It looks like a mess. I can't get the skin tone right, no matter what I try. It looks like I'm just painting on a different kind of nail polish. I consider a google search. Maybe that will help me get the nails to look how I want, but even if I do that will be on the photos I post. It will be clear that I'm wearing nail polish in all the photos that everyone else posts.

I decide it isn't worth it to mess with and leave it. It's for the best. I did like how it looked. I thought I looked cool with my tank and ripped jeans. The nails with the rings added this kind of edge that I really liked. Nothing's changing that.

I settle on a few photos of myself that look really cool and decide to post them to my Instagram with the caption *night one done* and a string of emojis. I hit post before I can think too much about it. The likes and comments flood in almost immediately, and that is one thing I will never get used to.

I don't want to scroll through them just yet, the notifi-cations are getting overwhelming. Instead, I decide to scroll through my mentions and the stories I've been tagged in, watching videos of us from the night and reposting a few stories. We looked good and sounded even better. I should have been proud of us. I *wanted* to be proud of us, but I had my father's voice in the back of my mind, and I couldn't get it to go away.

Chapter Two

The next morning in my hotel room, I wake up somehow still exhausted. I looked to the other bed in the room, Finn's bed, only to find it empty and the shower running. With a long drive ahead of us, and a show tonight, we had to be up early and take breakfast on the road.

Even at such an ungodly hour in the morning we were all thrumming with excitement. New York City was one of my most anticipated stops of the tour and I was eager to get on the road.

We load up the van with all of our suitcases, moving like excited and exhausted zombies and Finn smoothly pulls out of the parking space and begins to make their way to the highway. I can't imagine navigating this large van is easy, but they make it seem so easy behind the wheel. Every now and then they reach for their own coffee, a black iced, and I grimace.. It must taste disgusting. I could never.

Finn has music playing softly as everyone dozes in the back of the van.

"I don't understand how you can actually drink that," I say, eyeing the cup suspiciously.

"I just like it, princess," they say with a smirk, and there I am, staring at their lips again before directing my eyes back up to theirs hoping they didn't notice how badly I wanted to kiss them. "I just heard that only cool people drink black coffee, guess you're not as cool as I thought."

"Sorry to disappoint."

"You know I thought you had pretty good taste, I'm hurt." Finn gives me the most exaggerated pout.

"Yes, because my taste is the one that needs to be questioned right now."

"Your taste always needs to be questioned." Finn starts laughing and I can't help but smile.

"Can you please shut up? Some of us are trying to sleep," Aspen grumbles from her seat.

"And come on, we all Kyle has no taste so why are we even talking about it?" Harper adds curling into Aspen's side.

"Wow everyone's grumpy this morning, huh?" I look at Finn who seems just as tired as the rest of us. The comment only earns me a smack in the back of the head from either Aspen or Harper. "I'm just trying to help keep our driver awake, but it seems their bean juice is doing just that."

"Kyle, you did not call it bean juice." Finn shakes their head, and I can't help but notice the small smile that appears on their lips. *And I'm staring at their lips again.* I need to stop. Like now.

"Why are we even friends with this idiot?" Mari asks

from the back of the car. "Can we send him home and do the rest of the tour without him?"

"Mari shut up, you love me." I laugh.

"Guess we'll have to start holding auditions for a new guitarist…" Mari snickers as Aspen giggles.

"Okay, but can we please all shut up so we can sleep. I'm begging you," Harper says unamused. I look to Finn who shrugs and begins to quietly hum along to the music they're playing as they drive.

I stare out the window for a little over an hour before I too end up falling asleep, jolting awake when we pull off the highway to stop for gas. Everyone else gets out with a desperate need for the bathroom and snacks, the doors slamming shut waking me.

"Hey sleepyhead," Finn says as I climb out of the car. "Did you know you snore?"

"I do not snore," I counter.

"Come on, I know for a fact it wasn't any of the girls."

"And how are you so sure about that?"

Finn rolls their eyes at me. "I was sitting right next to you, and it was not quiet."

"Okay, but we all know your spatial awareness is shit," I joke, knowing that was a total lie.

"Then why am I the one driving?" They smirk.

"Do you want me to take over? You can get a nap in too."

"Nah, I think I'd be more scared to have you driving."

"If Kyle drives, I'm ubering the rest of the way," Mari says as she approaches us. "I'd rather pay for that than risk my life in the car with him."

"I'm not that bad of a driver!"

"You're not that good either. Stick to the passenger

seat. And maybe try not to fall asleep, you sound like a fucking jackhammer!"

"Oh, come on. I do not snore!"

"I wouldn't be too sure of that, but we'll record you next time." Finn grins." I could even record you tonight if I wanted to."

Aspen and Harper come join us outside the van, tossing me a bag of peach rings and Finn a bag of sour gummy worms.

"Sour gummy worms and black iced coffee. What am I going to do with you?" I laugh and glance at Stevie sitting in the back of the van working, but she's staring right at me, challenging me. I know I should back down, I should stop this back and forth that Finn and I have had going for years because she's their girlfriend and she doesn't like it. But I can't. There's something in the way they look at me when we're poking fun at each other that is special to me.

"You got a problem with that?" Finn winks at me and I can't help but melt a little.

"I'm starting to feel like maybe I should. Are you sure you're okay? Do we need to call someone for you? Maybe you've had too much caffeine. You didn't even eat breakfast. Don't you want like, real food?" I reach out a hand and playfully place it on their forehead. If Stevie could glare harder, I'd melt. But I am not backing down. She can be as possessive as she wants, but Finn is still one of my best friends and our relationship, our friendship, changes for no one.

Finn bats my hand away, laughing in a way they've never laughed with Stevie, at least not that I've seen. This laugh, the laugh that I'm getting, is the laugh I know they're too embarrassed to show in public. They sound like a dying duck, and I say that with love. "The gummy worms are my breakfast, thank you very much. I didn't realize that was going to be a problem."

I opened my mouth to respond before getting cut off by Stevie.

"You can have this conversation while we drive, as long as you're done getting gas." I've gone too far and pissed her off. Or she's getting territorial. Or maybe that's the same thing. I sigh and climb back into the van as we head back to the highway.

We're all a little more awake as we drive the rest of the way to New York City. Finn turns the music up and we relax into each other's company, enjoying spending time together. We sing along at the tops of our lungs until we pull up to the venue, then it's go time.

We pop out of the van and start pulling our instruments and equipment, going in and out of the stage door as we set everything up. We have six hours until the show and there's a lot that needs to be done. Things are being plugged in and rearranged and reorganized until we have the stage exactly how we want it. Then we jump into sound check.

We test our microphones and our instruments to make sure they sound exactly how we want and need them to. It takes a while and it's boring. It's a lot of standing around and waiting, getting to play one little bit or sing for a second and then going back to waiting until we're asked to do it again. The only fun part is when we get to play parts of our songs together so we can hear how they sound with all of us at once, and then things can be adjusted from there. It gets to be tedious and tiring real fast, but once it's done we get to head to our dressing rooms for a bit before the show.

Just like the hotel rooms, our dressing rooms are split up by gender. Sort of. It's Mari, Aspen, and Harper in one room and Finn and I in the other. Which works for me. It means more time spent alone with Finn. I shouldn't be wanting all this alone time, all this attention, from Finn when they are in a happy relationship with someone else. I shouldn't even be thinking about sabotaging that. They're my friend. I should want them to be happy.

We only get an hour after sound check to get situated in our dressing rooms and get some lunch before we have a meeting with one of the executives from our record label. It was a bit nerve wracking, going into the meeting. In a way, it felt like this man held our careers in his hands and he could do whatever he wanted with us.

I decided to quickly lay out my outfit for the show that night before heading out into New York City for a quick bite to eat before the meeting. If I had more time, I would have loved to explore the city on my own, or with the band, but out of respect for everyone's time I knew it would be best for me to be super quick and grab food from the first place I could find before rushing back in time for the meeting.

I ran into the room where the meeting was being held moments before the record label people walked in. They were all big men in suits, and it was a bit scary to see so many of them coming into the room. They all looked so serious, and I found myself sitting on my hands trying to hide the remnants of the nail polish that I had tried to pick off my nails last night.

The men began to introduce themselves, but I couldn't pay attention or catch their names. I just smiled and nodded. The entire meeting went by in a blur, and I found it hard to focus. They were talking about all these big things like our contracts and obligations and using big words I couldn't understand so I just sat there and nodded until they left. The one thing I did understand was they wanted an album. And they wanted it by the end of the summer, before we all went to college. And from what they said it sounded like we didn't exactly have a choice in the matter.

Stevie spent the entire meeting sitting behind her computer stone-faced. Though we didn't really get along, I looked to her for guidance. What were we supposed to do here? How important was all of this? Could we even do it? Should we even do it?

Once the men had left us to sit and contemplate or whatever they seemed to want us to do, panic broke out among us. I tried to stay calm, but I barely understood what was being asked of us. Our EP had taken us over a year to write and record and produce, and sure we were doing that while we were in school which made it more difficult to some degree, but now we had three months to turn in a finished album? Our EP was five songs. They wanted a project that was nearly double the size in less than half the time.

Aspen was hyperventilating and Mari looked like she wanted to throw up. Finn looked nervous too, and at least I knew I wasn't alone.

"Okay, let's breathe, maybe take five minutes and then come back and start working on a plan," Stevie says calmly, trying her best to bring some order into the room. Everyone gets up and leaves and walks throughout the backstage area. Finn goes directly over to Stevie and talks to her in a hushed voice so I can't hear what they're saying to each other, but Finn definitely looks panicked with their eyes wide and hands shaking ever so slightly. As I sit and wait for everyone to take their break, I can't help but pull out my phone and open up my Instagram post from last night. I know that I'm not supposed to look at the comments. Everyone I've talked to about my social media and how I should be handling it now that I'm "famous" has made that very clear, but there's a part of me that wants to know what people think, and a part of me that is still hung up on what my dad said yesterday and if other people believe that too. Because I thought my nails looked really cool until he said something.

The first handful of comments aren't bad. There are a handful from people who were at the show and seemed to have a really good time. There are lots of comments about the show, a few asking about new music, and a bunch of compliments that definitely making me blush, but of course I find the one comment that is actually negative, and it sticks out to me, screaming at me: *what self-respecting dude paints his nails?* I try to keep scrolling, try to not let it bother me, try to move on, but there was something about the comment solidifying what my dad had said last night that made it feel all the truer. What was I even doing thinking it was okay to walk around like that? I didn't need to parade my queerness, I should have known better.

After ten or fifteen minutes everyone comes back into the room, and we all sit waiting for further instruction from Stevie. As our manager she's supposed to know what to do, I think, but she's normally just as clueless as we are. I know she's new to all of this too, and she's really only here because she's Mari's older cousin. Yet it still feels like she should maybe know just a little bit more to be able to actually guide and manage us.

"Okay, I know a lot was said and we don't need to make any big decisions right now. But I think that this is a good thing. The label wants an album which I know is a big project and it sounds scary but here's how I'm thinking about it. They want an album done a month after tour ends. Or somewhere around there. And this tour, this summer, is the only time all five of you are going to be together for a long period of time before you all head off to college and can only spend time together during school breaks. We can negotiate for a later deadline, but I think this is a great opportunity. However, we don't need to make a decision right now. We can give it some time. We can take a few days, but let's try to have a decision by Friday. Can we do that?"

We all nod and get up to go our separate ways to start getting ready for the show. We will be able to figure this out. We will be able to come to an agreement on how to move forward. It's just a matter of how.

Chapter Three

"So, we're really going to have to do this?" I ask Finn as we get back to our dressing room to start getting ready for the show.

"Yeah, I guess." They reply as I look at the outfit I've pulled out for the show, absentmindedly picking off the remaining black nail polish still on my nails from the night before. "I mean, we've already started working on a few songs for it, all we're being asked to do is focus on it more. And besides, there's going to be a way for us all to work on it in different sections, right? Like teaming up or pairing off and working on songs to then take to the group as a whole. You know? It's not as bad as it seems when you break it down."

"You both think this is ridiculous, right?" Mari nearly yells, barging into our dressing room. "Do they really think we can actually produce a good album while on tour? It's insane." Mari sits on our couch with a huff.

"Dude, it's not that bad when you really think about it. Y'all are overreacting," Finn says dismissively as they start to unpack a few different bags with makeup and other things I don't recognize.

"You want to tell Aspen she's overreacting when she's hyperventilating on the floor? Be my guest." Mari shoots daggers at Finn with her eyes.

"That's not what I'm saying, and you know it. All I'm saying is it's completely doable and we should really consider at least trying it before we go and push back the deadline. And I know for a fact Stevie agrees with me."

"She only agrees with you because she's your girl-friend," I mutter while Mari looks downright pissed. "And if we do it she gets a nice payday."

"Since when is this all about the money? And what does her being my girlfriend have to do with it?" Finn crosses their arms as they take a step back.

"She's always been in it for the money," I say as I focus on picking off my nail polish.

"That's not true and you know it. You just don't like her. I don't understand what the problem is."

"This is more than me not liking her. Most of us here don't think this is something we as a band are capable of, but you're pushing for it and pushing her towards it. Aspen is literally having a panic attack and you think we can do this? You really think she's overreacting?" Mari yells.

"I don't understand why you're making such a big deal about it?" Finn says indignantly.

"It's such a short amount of time for us to be working on this. The EP took us forever and now we need to churn out an entire album over a few months."

"Right! Churn it out instead of actually working on it and giving it the time it deserves." Mari sighs and shakes her head. "Look, we'll all talk about this later, I guess. But please just really think about what this means for all of us." Mari storms out before we can get another word in.

Finn looks at me in disbelief, and I shake my head. With only half hour until the show, I decide to change into my show outfit.

"Kyle, stop picking off your nail polish. You're ruining all my hard work," Finn says as they put on some makeup. I look down at my hands in my lap and see the flakes of chipped polish all over my jeans and the lack of polish on my nails.

They put their eyeliner pencil down and look at me with a frown as they dig through one of their small travel bags, pulling out the same bottle of nail polish they used on my nails last night and a travel sized bottle of nail polish remover. "Come here, let me fix them."

Finn gets up and crosses the room over to where I'm sitting and grabs one of my hands gently, using the nail polish remover on a tissue to swipe off each little remnant of the polish that I had picked off.

"Maybe we shouldn't repaint them," I mumble, not even wanting to look up at Finn and see their disappointment. "I mean, if I'm just going to end up picking the polish off again is there really a point to wasting the nail polish?" I tried to justify the decision with the lamest excuse I could have come up with, but I couldn't help hearing my dad's voice in my head as I looked at the bare nails and thinking maybe he was right.

"Did you not like them, princess? I have some other colors, and I know Harper and Aspen brought all of theirs too, so if the color is the issue I can paint them a different color. I thought you really liked them. You were so happy when I painted them yesterday, did someone say something?"

"No, I just don't think it's the right look for me."

"Who said something?" Finn looks concerned and I want to shrink away from them just as much as I want to lean into them.. I want to tell them everything and feel them wrap me up in a warm hug and tell me everything's going to be okay, but at the same time I want to be able to move on from this.

"No one. I just don't think it's for me," I look down towards my lap, refusing to look them in the eye.

"I know you're lying. Kyle, tell me who said something. You were so excited for how cool it was going to look matching your black and red guitar and how badass it made you feel. So I'll ask you one last time: *who said something.*"

I sigh, pulling my hands back into my lap and avoiding eye contact like it's my job. "It was my dad. But really, it's not that big of a deal. I'm already on thin ice with him and he'll see the pictures and I don't want to make things worse. If I'm going to convince him to let me study music in college, I'm going to have to make some sacrifices for him and this is just one of them."

Finn's entire demeanor softens, and they grab my hands and force me to look up. "He isn't here. He's in a whole other state. You can't keep letting him control your life. You are so much more than what he thinks of you."

"I know. And I know whether or not I upset him shouldn't be so big of a priority... but, I don't know, he's still my dad. And he still has so much control over my life. Even though I'm away from home and about to move out and go to college, he chose the school I'm going to, he chose my major, hell if he could I wouldn't be surprised if he chose my friends. I don't get to have a choice in the matter."

"Kyle, it's your life."

"And right now he's the one footing the bill, so until I'm paying for everything myself, I have to follow his rules."

"Kyle—"

"Look, I get that your family loves you and accepts you and waves around a fucking rainbow flag all the time, but my family isn't like that. I'm lucky my dad has stopped being proudly homophobic. My mom supports me, I think, but she's scared of him. I mean, you've seen him."

Finn grabs my hand and stops me right in the middle of my thought.

"My family isn't all sunshine and rainbows like you seem to think. But your dad isn't going to see if you paint your nails. He's not going to look at every single picture you post and zoom in on your fingers. So if you want to paint your nails, then we'll paint them."

I look at them, and though everything in me is telling me that I shouldn't listen to them, that I should do as my father says, I still put my hand out and allow Finn to slowly slick on the paint. And when they're done and my nails are black again, I can't help but feel good looking down at my hands with the polish on. It just feels like me in a way I don't really know how to explain. It just feels *right*.

Before I know it, I'm tying my boots, tuning my guitar, and getting ready to head onstage for the second night of our tour. I feel a mix of nervous and excited energy flowing through me as I stand backstage waiting to go on. I bounce from foot to foot until it's time to go out onstage.

If I thought last night's crowd was loud, tonight's is even louder. I can't hear myself think in the best way possible.

It's wild, looking out into a crowd of people who are all there for you, or in my case, *us*, and watching them singing along to every word of every song. Every word we wrote, everything we created. Watching them dancing and háving the time of their lives... holy shit, it's intoxicating.

We get to the end of the first song in the set and the screams are deafening. And they don't stop. I stand there on the stage listening to the cheers of these fans who so badly wanted to be here with us tonight, and it doesn't feel real. I look to Harper who seems to be standing there, not knowing what to do. In all the shows we've played at local bars and coffee shops and whatever other venues we've gotten the chance to perform in, we've never had an audience reacting with this insane amount of energy.

"Holy shit." I mouth to Mari as the cheering continues to seemingly no end. We all look between each other in awe until Harper finally says into her microphone, "Holy shit! Y'all are insane!" that elicits more cheers from the audience.

I look to my microphone, desperately wanting to find something to say, anything that could even try to put into words how insane this is for all of us.

"So, tonight is only the second night of our tour and New York you are wild tonight! But I have to ask, are you ready for another song?" Mari calls into her microphone and I take that as my cue to come back to myself and prepare for the next song as the crowd cheers some more. "This is my favorite—Drama Queen!"

We launch into the song the second Mari stops speaking. I turn to Finn as we both jump on the punchy opening of the very upbeat song. Within seconds I'm fully in it.

For the rest of the show, I feel like I don't even have to think about what I'm playing, about what song comes next, what line, what chord, what note. I'm fully in the moment. I'm jumping around the stage with a boundless energy I don't think I've ever experienced before. It's new and it's exhilarating. Is this what it's supposed to feel like all the time? Is this why I'm trying to spend the rest of my life creating music?

All of a sudden, performing has become fun. The stage feels like my playground and I'm up there with my best friends. One of the coolest parts about it is that there's this large group of people who are in the room with us because something in our music resonated with them. They found something that they wanted to keep with them. Something that made them want to spend an evening with us.

After the show we get to hang out with some of the fans—it's still weird calling them *fans*. They're really cool people who like really cool music. If we had more time, I'd love to become friends with the awesome people who want to listen to the music we're creating.

A group of girls flock towards me as we're hanging outside the venue, trying to flirt while acting casual about it.

"You were amazing up there!" A tall blonde says with this really sweet, nervous smile.

"Thanks," I reply awkwardly. I wish I knew what to say. I wish someone had prepared us for this. Why can't I just talk to people? "Did you have fun?" I ask eventually, but it feels weird and wrong. The girls don't seem to notice.

"I think that might have been one of the best concerts I've been to!" One of the other girls in the group says with the biggest smile on her face. I look to Finn who's having their own conversation with a sweet looking girl. She seems so happy to be here in the most genuine way. I can hear her saying something about how much our music means to her, and I wish I was over there talking to her, standing next to Finn who looks fabulous tonight in the cropped band tee they decided to wear onstage, but instead I shift my focus back to the girls in front of me, knowing that's where my energy needs to be right now. The last thing I want to do is go on TikTok later and see a video about how I was rude to these girls. We don't need that.

"That was the best? You just saw Taylor Swift!" Her friend says with complete shock written all over her face. I laugh along with them before taking a picture. One of the girls at the last second decides it'll be cute to kiss me on the cheek. I try to smile and laugh it off as best as I can, but I feel weird.

I'm almost relieved when Stevie ushers all of us to the van, thanking the fans that have still stuck around, and getting us out of there. I slump into the back of the van, put my headphones in and start my relaxing playlist. Everyone's chatting and trying to come up with a plan for dinner, but I'm just tired. I want to head back to the hotel, take a shower and go to bed.

I pull out my phone after a few minutes of being stuck in traffic and open Instagram. I quietly scroll through posts and stories that I've been tagged in, looking for videos from the show. There's already a fan edit of a few videos of all of us reacting to the overwhelming cheers from the show. It's sweet. The sheer number of pictures and videos is overwhelming. It seems like there are new fan accounts popping up left and right. Every time I look there are at least five new ones. And they're not just from the states, they're from all over the world. The United Kingdom, Europe, Australia, and even some are popping up from Japan, Brazil, and countries so far away that traveling there never seemed like a possibility yet I'm constantly seeing comments asking when we're coming to their countries. Our music has this insanely wide reach and it's all thanks to social media. Maybe working on this album isn't such a bad idea. If we can figure out how to do it right, it could be really great. We just all need to be on board.

Chapter Four

When I finally get to the hotel room, I want nothing more than to crash. Performing has always been something I've loved, but it's also exhausting. I get to spend an hour-ish getting to run around a stage with my best friends. I'm constantly jumping and vibing on the stage in a way that feels so real and true to me, but now all I want to do is wash off the sweat and grime of the day and then climb into bed.

When I come out of the shower, feeling clean and in my sweats, I find Finn sitting on their bed. They've got the little pad of paper that hotels always seems to provide, humming something softly. They're so engrossed in whatever they're doing that they don't even look up as I walk back into the room.

They keep humming this really sweet melody over and over and it's really pretty. It has this really nice pull to it that has me wanting to fall into it.

"What if you brought it down at the end, instead of

up?" I suggest as they seem to be tinkering with this melody. They jump, startled by my voice.

"What?" They look at me, confused.

"Instead of the ending of that melody going like this…" I hum the melody they had been repeating ending on the higher note they were tinkering with. "What if it went down like this?" I hum it again, this time bringing it down to a lower note at the end giving this warm, almost melancholic feeling.

"Wait, I really like that!" They pull out their phone and shove it in my face with voice memos open. "Do it again."

I chuckle softly and then hum my revised melody into their phone. They play it out loud for themself to make sure they can hear it well, and then nod with a smile. I look over to the notepad and see what I can only assume are the beginnings of lyrics.

"Are you writing something?" I ask, genuinely curious but it comes out with a teasing lilt.

"Kyle, you should know I'm always writing something," they say with a smirk, pulling the notepad away from my prying eyes.

"You can't hide it now. You pulled me into this, it's our song now," I reach over and pulling the notepad closer to read some of the lyrics.

"It's nothing right now. Totally basic. The melody just like, I don't know, came to me. Is that weird? It feels weird to say, but it did. Like it just popped into my head, and I couldn't get rid of it, but the words aren't working." They look so defeated as they stare at the notepad.

"Firstly, that's not weird at all, I get it. I think that's just songwriting sometimes. But on the topic of lyrics, what are you trying to go for with this? Was there a specific vibe or something that you were going for? A topic you had in mind? I mean, everything you've written down seems very basic love song, which isn't a bad thing, but like it could maybe be deeper," I say with a hint of authority that I certainly don't have when it comes to this song. Or any song for that matter.

"Are you calling me basic?" They smirk and I swear I'm getting butterflies. What is wrong with me? They are one of my best friends and they are very obviously taken. This is not something I could pursue even if I wanted to.

"So, what if I am?" I stare them down for a second and will my heart to stop beating so fast.

They laugh, and it's that real genuine laugh that I love so much. It makes my heart soar. They never laugh like that in front of Stevie, or in front of anyone for that matter, it's special. Just for me.

"What are you trying to write about?" I try again, getting invested in the song in a way I hadn't expected to. It's like writing this song is a way into their brain, their psyche, and maybe, just maybe I can get in there and maybe even have a chance to make them mine even though I know it's a terrible idea. Dating someone you work with is always a bad idea, right?

"I don't know." They sigh, defeated. "I just wanted to write something that was all love-y dove-y for Stevie, I guess. I don't know, it sounds ridiculous when I say it out loud like that. I just wanted to write something to make her feel special."

Their words feel like a punch to the gut, and I try my best to keep from reacting. Or at the very least keep from reacting negatively. They want this song to be something special for their girlfriend. Of course they would. I shouldn't be hurt by that. I shouldn't mind it at all. So, why does it feel like someone's stabbed me in the heart?

"It's just lacking direction," I say pointedly. "You don't even know what you want to write. You don't have a path or a point or a focus. Are you writing about how she makes you feel? A special place the two of you went together? Your insecurities in the relationship? It needs more." I know I shouldn't have suggested that last idea, but if I can get inside their head and figure out where there are issues in their relationship, I can tear it apart from the inside. *No, that's awful.* They're my friend, and clearly, they're happy in this relationship.

"I guess you're right. Maybe I should sleep on it. Just figure out what I want, I guess. Figure out where I want to go with this. Unless you have any ideas. It is our song now. You get as much of a say in this as I do."

I lay back on my bed staring at the ceiling. "I don't know. There's something about writing about how much you love someone that feels, I don't know, boring? Overdone? I don't know. I feel like it needs to be raw, almost like it's a conversation between the two, in this weird way where we're only getting one perspective. I don't know, maybe that's too complicated. It feels complicated, and hard to write. So maybe not that. Maybe sleeping on it is a good idea, my brain feels fried."

"That's a cool idea though. I think I'm just struggling with the relationship." They say the words softly, hesitantly almost, and I can hear the pain in their voice. "Maybe it's the age difference, even though it's only two years I feel like she needs more of, like, everything. I'm not mature enough or I'm not tall enough, I'm not masculine enough, but not feminine enough in the same breath. It's stupid, I know, but like should we write about that?"

I'm silent for a while, almost too long, and I can feel them getting anxious next to me. I sit up and look at them sitting on their bed in a black oversized sweatshirt with their eyeliner from the show smudged and messy, and they look so fragile and tiny. How could anyone make them feel like that?

"That might be something for you to work out on your own. I'm not sure it's my place to help you write that. Get those feelings out onto the page and work out how you feel about all of it."

I look at them and I swear I see tears shining in their eyes and I want to get up and hug them and keep them from feeling this way. But I'm stuck, frozen on the bed. They just opened up and gave me the in I had been looking for, but I know I can't use it. I don't want to see them so hurt, even if it would give me the perfect opportunity to waltz in and save the day. I wouldn't get to be the hero. I'd be the worst friend. The villain.

And I need to think about what's in the band's best interest too. If Finn and Stevie were to break up, what would that do to our dynamic Stevie's our manager. She is in control of all of us. If I were to get in between the two of them, she could make my life hell. Would I be able to handle that? She could make music, the one thing I love more than life itself, my own living hell. She's the only reason Mari and Aspen could get their parents to agree to let them go on tour. We need Stevie here. At least for the tour.

I instinctively check my phone, only to see it's well past midnight and I have a string of unanswered texts from my dad. How long had we been working on the song? It had barely been eleven when I got out of the shower.

I hadn't actually posted any of the photos or videos from the show on my feed yet, we were waiting on the professional photos from the show, but I had reposted a few stories from fans who were there and my dad had seen them. Of course he had. And of course he wasn't happy.

Dad

DAD

[photo]

I thought we talked about this.

Is this really the image you want to be putting out to the public?

Future employers are going to be able to find these pictures.

Is that really what you want?

I thought you were better than this.

I sigh reading the messages. He's probably right. I know that. I should've listened to him. How many times is he going to tell me that music isn't going to be a stable career for me before I actually listen? How many times is he going to berate me until I give in?

KYLE

It's just nail polish

I know sending that is risky. I know he's not going to take it well. I know he's set in his ways, whatever they are, and that there's nothing I can say or do that will change his mind. I know better. I've spent the past eighteen years living under his roof. I know the right things to say and do and how to act to not stir up shit. But it's like there's something inside of me that just needs to stir this shit up. That needs to press his buttons. And it's not like I'm home. It's not like he can actually do anything about it. Right? He might threaten to come out here and pull me from the tour, but he wouldn't. Would he? Even though I am an adult I wouldn't put it past him to drive or fly out to wherever we are and pull me from the tour the second he doesn't like where things are going. And I would have to let him. Even after this tour, I don't think I would have enough money to really live on my own. I still need him.

DAD

Kyle Alexander Fishman you know it's more than that.

You are sending a message out to the world.

Presenting yourself in a way that will give people ideas.

Is that really what you want to do?

I raised you better than this.

He's angry and that's clear. I've done the one thing I'm good at—disappointing him. And now I know if I talk to my mom, or literally anyone for that matter, I'll be told to just appease him and say or do whatever I know will make him happy. Even though it hurts me. I just need to obey. It's the only way he's going to let me continue on like this.

Maybe if I please and appease him enough he'll allow me to study music business in college. Maybe he'll even allow me to transfer to a school out in California like I really want to. But I have to deserve it.

KYLE

I'll take it off

I send the text and throw my phone down on the bed. I'm already exhausted and dealing with my father has drained me of what little energy I had left.

Chapter Five

"Shit. Shit. Shit!" Finn exclaims as they pull over on the side of the highway, an hour from the venue, and waking all of us up.

"What'd you do?" Mari mumbles from the backseat, not even opening her eyes.

"We blew a tire. Fuck!" Finn says as they get out of the van and circle around it, looking at the damage. I hop out of the van too to try and help. I don't know how to help, or what to help with, but I know I want to help.

"How'd you manage that?" Stevie asks, sounding slightly pissed, as if Finn did this intentionally.

"I don't fucking know!" They sigh and look as if they're on the verge of tears. "It just happened!"

"These things don't just happen. What did you hit?" Stevie grills.

"*I don't fucking know!*" Finn repeats. "Please tell me we have a spare and that someone in this van knows how to change a tire."

"Shouldn't you?" Stevie sneers. "Not that you could

anyway, we didn't have enough room for all the equipment and the spare tire, so I left it in Boston."

"Oh great! You left it in Boston. So, what do you want us to do now?" Finn's seething. Stevie knows exactly how to push them.

"Shouldn't you know that?" Stevie says, not even looking up from her laptop.

"You're the fucking manager! Isn't knowing what to do and how to fix this shit kind of your job?" Finn pales as Stevie closes her laptop and gets out of the van.

"What, you just expect me to fix this for you? Fix all your problems until you're perfect? Is that what you want?" Stevie's practically yelling, and I can see Finn shrink in on themself. Is this what they were talking about last night when they said they felt like they weren't enough for her? Is this really how she thinks she can talk to them? How bad of an idea is stepping in? Like, I don't want to get involved. Or maybe that's not right. I want to get involved. I want to defend Finn. They deserve someone who's coming to their defense, not someone who is attacking them instead of helping them. But I shouldn't get involved, right? I should let whatever this is be between the two of them. It's not my relationship, it shouldn't be my problem. But then I see the way Finn looks so defeated and I just want to scoop them up and take them away from this mess.

"Isn't there some roadside assistance or something we could call to come and help us here?" I say trying to come between Finn and Stevie and whatever hell of a mess this is as I stand by Finn's side. They can have their own relationship issues when it's not going to cause us to be late to our own show.

"Is there a specific one you normally call or that will get here fast? I can look up a few if we need and I can start calling and see who can get here the fastest." Harper volunteers, only to get a dirty look from Stevie.

"Finnley made this mess, they can fix it," Stevie grabs her laptop and sits on the side of the road, opening it back up to do God knows what.

"Woah, this is no one's fault. We can help, it's not like we're doing anything," Mari jumps to Finn's defense before I have the chance.

"How is this not their fault?" Stevie asks, practically yelling. "They were driving. If I was driving this never would have happened!" Finn looks towards the ground, and I swear I can see tears in their eyes.

"You can't be so sure of that! These things just happen! And Finn's right, you're the manager, you're supposed to have the solution. You're supposed to fix this. So, fix it instead of yelling at them. That's not getting anyone anywhere!" I explode, hating how I have to just sit and watch Finn be berated. If anyone asks, it's because they're my friend and I really care about them. Nothing more than that. It's not because all I want to do is go run off into the sunset with them and make everything okay.

Harper walks back over to where the rest of us are standing by the van, and I hadn't even realized she had left. "I just got off the phone with three different roadside assistance companies nearby while you were all fighting, and someone should be here soon. You're welcome," she says, and I think it's safe to say we're all not feeling the best about Stevie right now. Not that I think there's something we can do about her. At least not while we're on tour, right? I mean, she has all of the information that we need to be able to get through this whole thing.

It's then, as we're all standing out in the heat waiting for someone to come and fix this that I realize we haven't heard a peep from Aspen. I look to the grassy area where everyone's taken to sitting while we wait, and I don't see her over there. I look around the general area, hoping she's not in the hot van or planning to walk into traffic while everyone else seems busy on their phones or doing whatever they're doing to pass the time, and find her walking, almost pacing, not too far from the van. She's far enough away to get a bit of a break from the group and the fighting, but not far enough that we can't see her.

I slowly walk over to where she's pacing, only bumping up my pace to a jog when I'm sure the rest of the band isn't watching or even aware.

"Hey. Are you okay?" I ask, though to any of us it should be very clear she's not.

"It's already been half an hour. We were supposed to get there in half an hour," she mumbles and I can tell she's doing everything she can to remain calm. "The venue is expecting us. And we're supposed to be there. And we're going to be late. And we don't even know how late. We're supposed to have sound check in two hours. We don't know how long it's going to take for someone to come fix the damn van. We could be stuck here for four hours, and it's not like the next nice stranger that decides to stop and ask if we're okay can just drive us to the venue. Not that we should trust that anyway, but we have all this equipment we need and if we're super late, then we don't have time for a proper soundcheck, the show could go awfully, and then our fans will hate us, and we'll lose our followers and then the label will drop us and then…"

I do the only thing I can think of and just pull her into a hug. I've seen this time and time again with my best friend Aubrey and her anxiety. I know, for the most part, what to do.

"First, I need you to breathe," I say once she's stopped talking and I've pulled away. I know the one thing I really need to do is pull her out of this spiral and get her back to the present.

She nods, but I can see her struggling to take a full deep breath.

"Okay, just try to follow my breathing. Try to copy me." I focus my breathing, taking nice deep breaths. I hold eye contact with her the entire time as she takes a handful of shuddering breaths before she manages to match my breathing.

I smile as she starts to calm down. "Good. You're doing great. Just keep breathing. You've got this." I keep her hands in mine and my eyes on hers. "I know this is a very stressful situation. There's so much here that's out of all of our control. But we need to focus on what we can do right now," I say as I wrack my brain trying to think of anything we could do.

"There's something we can do? Other than just sit around and wait?" Aspen asks, seeming truly baffled by the idea.

"There's got to be something. I know there's something. We can fill this time, somehow." I look back to where the rest of the band is sitting, and I know there's something we should be doing. Something we can be doing that will get us to pass the time. "We can work on the album. I know the side of the interstate isn't the best place to work on writing a song, but I can pull out my acoustic guitar and we can start working on something. There was that song we were working on over spring break?" I suggest, but when I look at Aspen, she just looks even more panicked.

I turn Aspen away from the rest of the band, walking her back in the other direction to where the rest of the band is sitting on the grass on the side of the highway as cars fly by. "The album's making you anxious, isn't it?" I ask gently. Am I even doing this right? Is this even helping or am I making it worse by asking stupid questions?

"It's just, we spent so much time on the EP and now we're expected to spend half that amount of time on an album? It just feels like a lot."

"It is a lot. You are completely right about that. But here's the thing, we were in the middle of high school during the entire process. We needed more time. We had schoolwork and extracurriculars and sports and lives."

"I know. I've heard it a million times. Everyone keeps saying the same thing. But it still feels like this massive undertaking that I'm just not sure is possible. Is that crazy? I mean, I know it's crazy, but like, we have one half written song. And we need what, twelve more? By August? There's only five of us, and songwriting has always been so collaborative for us."

"I'm not saying any decision needs to be made today, let alone right now. But there are other ways to think about it. And whether or not our deadline is in a week, a month, or even a year, we'd be using this free time to work on our music because that's just who we are as a group. It's always how we've functioned. All through high school, every time we were getting together to rehearse or make videos for social media, we would end up spending at least an hour writing or working on something. It's how we've always worked. So, all we need to do is amp that up."

She looks at me with this defeated look and I can't help but feel guilty that I've made her feel that way. "We can work our asses off and still not get it done by the end of tour and that's okay. I'm sure all the label really wants to see is that we're actually working on something and that we're taking this seriously. I think their plan might be to get it out over our winter breaks so we can do press for it all together before we have to go to school. But that's not something we have to worry about now."

Aspen starts to relax and nods looking almost hopeful. "You really think they won't be mad if it's not perfect by the end of summer?" she asks and there's a flicker of hope in her eyes.

"Yeah. I'm pretty sure if they just have an idea as to what we're going to be putting out when we all go off in our own directions, they'll be happy with whatever we've got. I'm sure they'll be understanding." I smile at her and the way she completely relaxes helps me relax too. I've done something right. I've helped. And I've maybe just gotten another person on Finn's side. That should make Finn happy, right?

The two of us walk back over to where the rest of the band is sitting on the grass. Harper's sitting on her phone, probably scrolling through social media, as is her favorite way to spend any amount of downtime. Stevie is still typing away on her laptop, totally oblivious to the world around her, and Mari looks like she's napping. I'm honestly not surprised. That girl can sleep anywhere. And Finn… they look like they've been crying, with their red rimmed, puffy eyes, and my heart breaks knowing I couldn't do more to help them.

I walk to the back of the van and open up the trunk, pulling out my acoustic guitar, and then sit next to Finn with the guitar on my lap and my phone open. I refresh my mind with what was written back in March and start fiddling around with it on guitar. Harper immediately starts humming the melody absentmindedly and I can't help but smile as I begin to mess around with the bridge that we had started working on but hadn't really figured out just yet.

I start playing around with the chords and the beat that we might want to use. Trying different ways of strumming them, trying to figure out what we might want the vibe of the bridge to be.

"I really like that," Harper says after I play something super soft and slow, not even looking up from her phone. "Can you play it again?"

I pull up the voice memos app on my phone and hit record before playing it again. Harper immediately starts messing around with words, and I go back to my notes app looking at what we had for lyrics when we had worked on it before. We hadn't really come up with much for the bridge at that point, other than a few lines here and there. It wasn't much at the time, but as we sat waiting for someone to come and change the tire, Harper and I seemed to find the groove in the song.

At some point, Finn had gone to the bus and pulled out their drumsticks. Though figuring out their part of the bridge wouldn't work too well without the physical drum set, but they still managed to write notes for themself as they drummed on the concrete. Of course, we'd still have to work on the bass line and keys part later, when we have access to everything, but it was nice to be able to write at least part of the song before the first roadside assistance truck pulled up to change our tire. We were an hour away from the venue and we need to be on in an hour and a half. If this show actually runs smoothly it will be a miracle. But we can only hope for the best.

Chapter Six

We got back in the van and we were off, driving as fast as possible without speeding, trying our best to get to the venue with enough time to spare. Harper, Aspen, and Mari all tried their best to put on whatever makeup they could in the back of the van while making sure they didn't stab their eyes out, which was a genuine concern. I had never thought of makeup as being dangerous but then Mari showed me how sharp her eyeliner is and how it needs to get really close to her eyes, and sometimes has to even go in her eye? She tried explaining it to me, and you'd think I'd actually have a better understanding of makeup because I'm gay, right? But none of it made sense. And even if I did spend the time to actually learn what all the different products she puts on her face are, and learned how to do it in a way I would like on my own face, I'd never hear the end of it from my dad.

Which reminds me: I need to take off the nail polish before tonight's show. But that's not something I can do in the van. Apparently, the remover smells really bad and will stink up the entire van and give Stevie even more of a headache than she already has.

When we arrive at the venue it's go time. We all hop out of the van and immediately start running things into the venue to set up. We're running back and forth like crazy, and the line of fans waiting to get into the venue is already down the block. The venue was supposed to open the doors half an hour ago. We're way behind.

We get to pop on stage for about two minutes for soundcheck before rushing back to the dressing room to get ready. I quickly threw on whatever outfit I could find first and hoped I looked decent before quickly making sure my guitar was in tune and grabbing my in-ear monitors before heading to the stage with Finn right behind me.

Of course, as we got to the stage, nerves were high for all of us.

To no one's surprise, the show starts out incredibly rough. We get out on stage and start playing, but I can't hear any of my cues or even the rest of the band in my in-ear monitors. I can't even hear myself. I immediately pull one out and focus on what I can hear in the venue, but from my spot on the stage I'm struggling to hear anything. In the rush of everything, something certainly didn't get plugged in correctly.

And then I go to sing some sort of harmony into my microphone and the first time I do it, not a single person in the venue can hear it. Of course they can't, right? Then the second time it is far too loud. Maybe I was trying to be louder than I normally am. That could be part of it, but it completely drowns out Harper.

When we try to do introductions it's a hot mess. I try to

look off stage to find Stevie and see if she can get on it, but she's nowhere to be found. Of course.

I look to the audience, trying to gauge just how bad it sounds to them, and a few fans are wincing while others look pissed. I'd be pissed too if I was expecting a good show and paid to come to this mess.

Finn tries to really lean into their microphone as we start the second song of our set. They try to brush off counting all of us in, and counting in every different verse and chorus as being something we do during the show, but they were just trying to keep us on track.

From what I could hear, the second song sounded better for the audience, but not by much. I keep looking off stage to try and find Stevie, but she's nowhere to be found. And I'm getting frustrated. How did she just disappear when we need her the most?

We try to stall before our third song, trying our best to give the sound techs some time to get everything set up for us so we can have a smooth rest of the show, but it seems none of our monitors are plugged in by the time we start the third song. And it's awful. I don't know if I should be blaming the venue or us. We were late, sure, but aren't we all professionals?

Finally, as the third song comes to an end, I look offstage and see Stevie walking into the wings, looking disheveled, with one of the sound techs trailing on her heels. After the day she's had I only want to assume she's been yelling at him and ripping him a new one. Yet she somehow doesn't look as angry as she had earlier. What changed? What did this sound guy have to say?

I'm finally able to make eye contact with her, and as the fourth song is being introduced, I point to my ears and hope I'm getting my message across. She looks confused at first, so I point again and shake my head. But that still doesn't get the message across. So, I quickly run offstage to tell her that none of our in-ear monitors are working. I ask her to check if they were plugged in before running back onto the stage and hoping it gets fixed.

And magically, just as we start our fourth song the monitors start to work. The five of us, while standing onstage, let out a collective breath and the rest of the show is able to run smoothly. Luckily.

We get off the stage to a very angry Stevie. Videos from the start of the show are already circulating on the internet and even though none of this was our fault she seems to want to blame all of us. No, not all of us. She's still on some power trip convinced this is all Finn's fault.

"What the hell was that?" she yells the second all five of us are offstage. "Videos are already all over social media. Do you know how bad this looks for you? People paid good money to be here for you to give some half assed, awful sounding show. I know you're just kids, but you are professionals. You know better."

As she yelled at us, I was seething, vibrating with a deep anger all towards her. "I think we handled that professionally considering you were nowhere to be found," I snap.

"Are you saying it's my fault? Because the last time I checked, Finnley was the one to pop the tire." She sneers and Finn shrinks in on themself. Finn didn't do shit. She has to know that. Right?

"The tire was no one's fault," I say immediately, trying to stand up for Finn as best as I can. "However, our in-ears not working properly was someone's fault. And the fact that we were nearly halfway done with our set was the real problem. The fact that you either couldn't tell something was wrong or just weren't around was the problem."

"The problem was that someone had to make us late. If we had gotten here on time, like we had planned, none of this would have happened."

"Maybe if you had planned better, we wouldn't have had to worry about our timing when it came to an auto issue that was completely out of our control. Or, I don't know, maybe if you hadn't gotten rid of the spare tire, we could have just figured out how to change the tire ourselves and maybe be an hour late instead of four," Mari yells and I don't know if I've ever seen her so angry. But of course, we were all going to be running to Finn's defense.

"Actually, I think we might just need someone else to do the driving. Give Finnley a break and maybe show them how driving should be done while they just sit and watch. Maybe that way you can actually learn how to do things properly."

I gasp softly hoping no one hears. Was she really trying to treat Finn like they're a child? Is that really her solution?

"Are you actually trying to punish me?" Finn asks, a look of pure shock spread across their face.

"You're going to need to learn somehow, aren't you?"

"Then go for it. You drive for the rest of tour."

"I've got plenty of work to be doing during the drives."

"Then who else is going to do it? Aspen doesn't have a license, no one trusts Kyle, Mari won't drive for that long, and I know Harper really doesn't want to. So, I volunteered because I really don't mind driving. But if my driving isn't good enough for you, then you should do it. Besides, if this is really how you feel about me then maybe

I shouldn't be so forgiving after you so clearly fucked the sound guy in the janitors closet during our first few songs. Again." Has this happened before? And why did Finn decide to forgive her the last time? None of this is okay at all, why would they even want to put up with that?

"His name is Josh," she says, getting defensive as if what she had done was in any way right. I look between Finn, Stevie, and the rest of the band. Mari looks like she's wants to scream at her cousin, while Harper and Aspen are just trying to look away and not be part of this moment.

"Well have fun with *Josh* or whoever it is in the next city, because I'm done," Finn says and storms out, leaving all of us in shock. I immediately got up and started running after them. I don't know why, but I know I have to clean up this mess.

I know I shouldn't be happy right now. And I'm not. I'm definitely not. Have I wanted Finn and Stevie to break up? Of course I have. Have I wanted it to be slightly messy so I could swoop in and save the day while sweeping them off their feet in the process? Who wouldn't? But I also know that in my idealized version of whatever this was going to be, Finn wouldn't be hurting at any point within this mess. They would be ready for something with me.

Rushing into something with Finn, if they even wanted to, would be just as messy. We'd be risking the future of the entire band and everything we've been working towards by getting together, especially if it ended badly. Not that I think that a relationship with Finn will end in flames, but it is a possibility I would have to consider for the sake of the band. We've all been working so hard, and we're only going to grow from here, right? That's the goal anyway. We all have big dreams: major awards, headlining festivals, stadium tours, major collaborations, all of it and then some. Would pursuing this relationship put that all at risk? Would it be worth it?

I follow Finn to our dressing room. I stand outside the door for a few minutes. Should I even be going in? Should I give them space? Do they just want to be alone, or would it be okay if I joined them in the room?

I go in anyway and find them curled up on the couch, crying. They look up when I walk in and it's the first time I allow myself to just walk right over to the couch and scoop them up in my arms. I hold them while they sob. I don't say anything. There's nothing I can say. All I can do is try to support them in the best way possible. All I can do is be here.

After a few minutes, I pull away and they hop up off the couch and start to pack up their suitcase, packing whatever they had taken out to get ready for the show in the limited time we had in the venue before rushing onstage.

"Are you quitting?" I ask timidly as they furiously pack the makeup that was strewn about one of the tables. I didn't want to ask the question, didn't want to even think of it as a possibility, but the hard truth is that they could decide they need to leave this tour. Right now. And I know I wouldn't be able to stop them.

"What? No! Oh my God! Of course not! Did I give you the impression that I was going to quit? I could never do that to you and the rest of the band. We've all worked too hard for this for me to just up and quit after a few shows."

"Oh." Even though it's what I wanted to hear, it wasn't what I had been expecting. We don't have a choice but to keep working with Stevie, at least until we finish this tour, which means Finn would have to be stuck with her. Plus, after the way she's been treating them, I don't think any of us want to be around her more than we absolutely have to be.

"Looks like you're stuck with me. Sorry to disappoint." Their smirk returns to their face for just a minute, and I can't help but melt the tiniest bit. That smirk is my favorite. It comes with the twinkle of their eyes, and you'd miss it if you weren't looking for it, but when they're teasing me it's always there. Just for me.

"What makes you think I'm disappointed?" I reply with a teasing lilt to my voice. "Do you really think I'd want to have to rush to find a new drummer on such short notice? And besides, we have a song to finish."

"Right, the song. How could I forget that you've completely taken over and decided it's yours now?"

"Not mine. *Ours.*"

"Right. Ours." They smile at me again and despite their red, puffy eyes I think we're both finally hopeful that this is going to be okay.

They continue to pack up all of their things, and it's shocking to see how much mess they've made in the fifteen minutes we spent in here before the show.

"I don't know if this is going to help at all but," I say after a few minutes of silence, hating how awkward it feels. How am I supposed to just exist in this room with them, while they're clearly so upset and newly single, and not do anything about it? I know I shouldn't. But if what they said when we were working on that song the other night was any indication, Stevie's been treating them like that for a while and they just never had the courage to say anything. What was I doing wrong as a friend that they felt they couldn't come to me with that?

"Stevie's kind of awful. And after this tour is over, we can fire her and find a new manager." I hope that this could at least be slightly helpful. I want nothing more than to be saying things that can be found helpful. There's this overwhelming need to just know that they like me, and maybe even want me, in the way I so desperately want them. It's ridiculous really. We're friends. I know they like me. We wouldn't be friends if they didn't like me. But I just want to know that this can go deeper. *We* can go deeper.

"Thanks," they say softly, putting down the t-shirt they're folding.

"I know I can't speak for everyone," I begin hesitantly, "but I hated the way she was treating you. She was just awful and you didn't deserve that. You're amazing, truly, and I'm sorry she couldn't see that." I look to them and see the tears in their eyes again and can't help but feel slightly guilty. Had I said something wrong?

"Thanks," they say again, though this time it comes out as more of a strained whisper. They wipe their eyes on the back of their hand and smile at me in that quietly reserved way that they always keep for me. Or at least that's what it feels like.

After a while there was a knock on the door and Harper stuck her head in. I could see both Aspen and Mari standing not too far behind her, Stevie nowhere in sight.

"Can we come in?" Harper asks tentatively. "It's just the three of us." I should've known they would come eventually. It should have been a given. We've always shown up for each other through break ups and deaths and whatever else we've all had to go through in the past few years, but a selfish part of me wanted to keep Finn to myself for just a little bit longer. But they need all of us, not just me. They need to be around their closest friends, which happen to be every single member of this band.

Finn nods and they all stand awkwardly by the door, as if they don't know what to do or how to hold themselves in this situation. Finn has never been one to come to us with their problems, even though we've always been super supportive of each other no matter what. And to a degree I get it, most, if not all of what they were going through these past few years, would not have been something we would have understood, but they always had our support nonetheless. So now when they absolutely need us, we're at a loss. But we will try our best and I guess that's all they can really ask for. Right?

"Are you okay?" Mari asks and immediately cringes. "Sorry, that's a stupid question. Of course you're not okay. Um, we were going to get dinner before heading back to the hotel if you wanted to join us, but it makes total sense if you don't want to. If I were you, I'd want to just leave and go home. But if it wasn't obvious we're all on your side. Just let us know what you need." Aspen and Harper nod along and when I look over at Finn to see how they're handling this they have the tiniest smile on their face. Maybe we are doing something right.

"Dinner sounds like a good idea. I could use the distraction. I just need to get my mind off of this," they say with a smile, slowly climbing off the couch to finish packing up the dressing room and get ready to go.

Chapter Seven

There's a weird routine for the next few days. I think if it was up to all of us, we'd avoid Stevie at all costs. No one wants to be around her. Finn especially, but I'm a close second. But that just wasn't something we were able to do. We have to work with her. We have to spend time with her. We have to be around her. She is still in control, whether we like it or not.

She also seems to not want to be around any of us. She doesn't talk to Finn unless she absolutely has to, and even then, she's asking some of us if we can relay messages for her so she can avoid them. I know she's hurt by all of this too, she is also going through a breakup, but I just don't understand how one person can be so mean to someone, especially Finn.

And it is so hard watching Finn struggle so much. I want nothing more than to pick them up and take them away from all this. I wish we could run away and go somewhere where none of this matters.

We've also gotten into a pretty solid routine when it comes to the shows. Finn's still driving us, though Stevie loves to make it known how bad of an idea she thinks it is. Half the time she's talking to or about Finn she's still so mean and negative towards them and I just hate it so much. No one should have to deal with a bully like her, but especially not Finn.

As the first week of the tour comes to an end, Stevie holds a meeting with us to discuss the potential of an album and discuss what we want to do. Well, she calls it a meeting, it's really lunch at a diner and she's cornering us into having this discussion against our will.

"So, I gave you a week to think about whether or not you want to pursue this album on a summer deadline. I want to hear from everyone. I want to hear everyone's thoughts, both positive and negative. I want any worries to be voiced and I want to come to a conclusion by the end of this meal," she says, all stern and businesslike. That seems to have been the only tone we've gotten from her all week long, not that I mind keeping this a strictly professional relationship, but it's just a big shift from what we've had.

"We'll go around the table in a minute, but first I do want to say that I think this is a really good idea. I think that all of you will really benefit from working on the album now, especially since you're all planning on going to college in the fall and the time spent together is going to be extremely limited come mid-August. I think that way we can try and plan for a late January release so you can then spend your winter breaks doing press for the album all together before going back to school for the spring semester. I think it would be stupid to put it off when you're all stuck with each other for the next two months with virtually nowhere to go. But I can't make this decision for you."

She's stern as she looks around the table looking for whoever is willing to start. None of us want to be doing this. Sure, we know that we need to come to a conclusion about this quick so we can decide how much time we're planning on investing into the album during the tour, but it's just not something we all really want to be thinking about.

"This tour is the most amount of time we'll be spending together at least until we graduate college," Mari starts, seemingly interested in the idea of pursuing this album after having time to really think it over. "I guess, my concern is more that we're all going to college and going off to start this next chapter of our lives and like what if this band stops being part of that?"

"What do you mean?" Harper asks, genuinely interested, though I want to think we all understand what Mari is trying to say.

"Like we're not going to be seeing each other every single day anymore, or like just as much in general, so like what if we all go off to college and decide we don't want to do this anymore? I don't want to lose everything we've been working so hard for. And I guess part of me feels like if we're working on this while we're in school then we'll have a reason to talk to each other." Mari is starting to get teary-eyed and emotional and a part of me aches to hug her and reassure her that everything will work out.

"We're not going to stop being friends because we're

going to college," Harper says and I know she's trying to be helpful, but I watch a tear roll down Mari's cheek.

"You say that now, but I've seen this before. All those girls I used to be friends with said the same thing when they went to college two years ago, but we're not. They stopped answering my texts. What if that happens between all of us? It is a possibility, and we can't rule it out." Mari's full-on crying now and it hurts my heart to see her so upset.

"Just because we're finished writing the album by the end of summer doesn't mean we won't still have work to do on it during the fall. There's still going to be production and things we're going to have to approve, we're going to have to work on a track list and deciding what songs just aren't going to make it and if we want to do a deluxe album. And then there's all the press we'll have to do leading up to the release and then afterwards and it's going to be so much work and so much that we'll have to do, but the thing is we'll have to do it together. It's going to be something we'll have to do together," Finn says as they grab Mari's hand.

Honestly, I hadn't even thought of that as a possibility. It had always been a given that we were going to stay friends and stay together no matter what. In all of my future plans, the band has always been there. This band is my career. This band is my future. Even if my father has other ideas, this band was always going to be a part of my life. And I would never let it just fizzle out because we all went to college. That simply will never happen. Never ever.

"I actually think this plan for the album is a really

streamlined way to work on it. If that makes sense," I say before anyone else has a chance to speak. "I mean, we're all together for the next two months. We're not going to be doing much else and we'll have plenty of time to work on this. Sure, we might have to give up days off, or work around them, or take less, but we'll figure it out. But when we go to college that's it. We're in college and we're not going to have the opportunity or time to really work together like we will now. We can plan things so that we're able to get together during school breaks to work on things band related while we're all home, and that means having to talk to each other somewhat regularly. The way I see it, this band is our future, it's our career, and we're stuck with each other and working on this album will just cement that further."

I look to my bandmates and see everyone nodding in agreement and maybe that's the smartest thing I've said all day, but if we're going to have some sort of future with this band we need to work for it. And I will. I'll do whatever it takes.

"I've been completely on board for working on this album since we were approached with this idea," Finn said, somewhat nervously. I could only imagine they were worried their opinion was not part of the majority. "I mean, this is the opportunity of a lifetime. Can we really pass this up?" I could feel Finn buzzing with excitement and I wanted to feel that way too.

"We're so young, our lives are just starting and we're being asked to work on a project like this. Sure the deadline might feel tight, but our label wants this from us. They see potential in us and a successful future for us, otherwise they wouldn't be asking for this. This band, as it is right now, is already blowing up. Social media is scary with all the new followers and comments and whatnot, but this is something I don't think we can let pass us by. We have to pursue this. I think it would be stupid not to." They sound so eager and excited and after a week where they were feeling so rough it's making me, and hopefully everyone else, just so excited to be working on this project.

"Right, doing this and then going on some sort of hiatus while we're in college for the next four years might not be terrible," Aspen says, a big smile spreading across her face and I can't help but think our conversation the other day had something to do with her excitement.

"And most of us will be in or near Los Angeles for college anyway," Finn adds.

"That is true," Harper said with a smile. "The only one of us that won't be is Kyle."

"And me," Mari says, her voice barely above a whisper. "I'm going to be taking a gap year and traveling around Europe. I just finalized the plan." Everyone goes quiet. This changes things. Mari being in Europe, traveling, and hopefully having the time of her life could make working together as a band this next year difficult.

"I think we can all agree that we've worked way too hard on this to just up and quit because we decided to go to college. We will find a way to make this work for all of us." Harper chimes in, trying to be optimistic.

"So, what I'm gathering is everyone seems to be on board for this. We all want to pursue this album for the end of summer deadline?" Harper asks, but I think the consensus is clear. "The only thing I'm unsure about is how we're going to write and record upwards of, I don't know, roughly fifteen to twenty songs in two months." We all look to Stevie for the answer.

"Not all five of you are going to be writing every song. Sure, there will be a few songs that each of you are writing, and everyone will get to edit and have opinions on all of the songs, but you're going to break off into pairs or write on your own and bring things to the group. I think that's going to be the fastest way for this album to get done. So, start stockpiling those ideas and go through all those old notes and voice memos of things that weren't used for the EP and see if there's anything there that you want to revisit. That's going to be a great place to start."

We go back to the hotel, and it isn't long before Stevie sends us all a new, very intense, schedule for the rest of the tour. Alongside all of the scheduled shows, interviews, photo shoots, and everything else she has had planned for us, she has now added studio and writing sessions and blocked off time nearly every day where at least a pair of us is working on something. To be fair to her, it is arranged well. She's planned it so that if two of us even have a moment of downtime we could be working on something, but that does mean she plans for us to almost always be working on or recording something. Our days off are now virtually nonexistent. Music is no longer just fun for us. It's our job and something we are all going to need to be working very hard on. We don't get to have a choice anymore. With Mari planning to spend most of the next year in Europe, we need to get as much done as possible while we're all together. But it doesn't matter. We get to treat music as a job because it is going to be our job. And that is what's important. That is what I need to focus on.

Back in the hotel room that night Finn and I sat on one of the beds, my acoustic guitar and a notepad in between us, trying our best to work on the song, but it wasn't working. At least not how either of us really wants it to. The song has quickly become a hard one for us to write. We're both looking for different things out of it,

If it was up to me, I'd be writing a song with Finn solely about how I feel about them. Maybe it would give them a hint as to how I feel. Maybe it would start something between us. Maybe we'd get to explore this love language of music through writing together.

But as I sit with Finn, I know it's not what they need. They need to write about everything that they're feeling. Everything they're going through. I want to help, of course, but at the same time, the last thing I want to be doing is helping Finn write a song about Stevie.

"I don't get it. Why isn't this working?" Finn says, frustrated, as I absentmindedly strum on my guitar. "I know what I want to say, why can't I get it to fit?"

"Maybe you need to step away from it for a minute," I say as I open my phone and check my last Instagram post. It's getting a fair bit of traction.

There are a few comments about the nail polish again. I keep forgetting to take it off. At least that's what I keep telling my dad every single time he mentions it, which is every single time I post something. I really should take it off. I don't need him to be so on top of me about it constantly, but every time I get onstage and look down at my hands and see the nail polish it feels right. I know that sounds stupid. It's just nail polish. It doesn't actually mean anything, but there is something about it that makes me feel more like myself than I have since I was a child, and nothing mattered.

"You're not even trying to help," Finn complains. "You keep saying this is our song, but you're just sitting there on your phone."

"Okay then, how can I help?" I say as I put my phone down and pick up my guitar. Honestly, I just have no idea what they want from me. Every single suggestion I've made in the past hour has been wrong. What am I supposed to do or say when nothing I'm saying is the right thing? "Do you want to go back to discussing a theme or idea? Maybe that'll help with the lyrics. Or we could play the melody again. What do you need?"

They sigh and flop back on the bed. "I don't know. I want to know what we need to make here."

"That couldn't be vaguer if you tried." I laugh, hoping they find it just as funny but knowing I'm probably on the wrong side here.

They roll their eyes at me, and I can't help but smile. "I don't know, princess. I just don't want to write about Stevie and about all that shit, but it's all I can think about. I just want to write something fresh, not all sad and 'I don't believe in love,' you know? But all I can think about is the end of a relationship that just hurts so deeply."

"What if you write both," I suggest. "Write it sort of like a duet. Almost as if there's this couple and one person is just madly in love with their partner, and the other wants nothing to do with the relationship. Or maybe it's like telling a story of a relationship from start to finish where you start out with all these feelings and motifs of being so in love and as the song goes on they're falling out of love."

"Like it's two sides of the same person fighting with each other?" They ask and they just look so hopeful, like they've finally gotten to a place with the song, with this idea, that has them just excited to get writing again, and I can't help but be excited for them and with them.

"Yeah exactly." I smile at them as they start to scribble something down on the notepad. They write for a few minutes before they even come up for air.

"Maybe it could even be about how in love I thought I was with Stevie even though all she did was tear me down." So, she was really like that all the time. She was just awful. And they put up with that. For months. How did none of us see it?

"She was like that all the time?"

"Not all the time, but yeah, she did that a lot. It's like her love language or something." They're starting to get defensive now. Maybe I'm crossing a line, but if it's all just out of concern I'm not really doing anything wrong, am I?

"So, she's just always been awful to you."

"I guess. It sounds really bad when you put it like that. It wasn't all bad." I should stop. I should drop this. They're practically pleading with me to drop it. But I can't. If it was anyone else, maybe, but not for Finn.

"I'll take your word for it, I wasn't there, but you deserve so much better. You could do so much better. I hope you know that." I can only hope that they can actually see it.

"Thanks. I appreciate that."

"Did she ever hurt you physically?" I ask tentatively. It's a big question, and I know that, but I need to know.

"No! Oh my God no!" They look at me with pure shock written across their face, as if my asking that had been so out of line. "She would never."

"I'm sorry, I had to ask."

"Can we just write the song? Please?"

I sigh and nod, turning back to my guitar. Clearly, I've crossed a line.

Chapter Eight

The next morning, or more like early afternoon, we were corralled into our dressing rooms to get ready the second we got to the venue. Even though it is hours before the show, we have an interview scheduled with a local news outlet to take place backstage. They were kindly coming to us, so we have to be dressed and ready to go as soon as they were in the building out of respect for their time and ours. So, we were rushed off to get ready and we needed to be dressed nice, maybe not to the full extent of what we'd be wearing on the stage, but something above casual.

I just put on what I would be wearing on stage that night: my favorite black ripped jeans, doc martens, and a random t-shirt. I debate taking off my nail polish or touching it up, but before I have a chance to make a decision, we were being pulled from the dressing rooms and brought into the room where the interview would be taking place.

Finn and I walk together, following behind the very

kind person who came to grab us, and took our seats next to each other on the two open spots left on the couch. We take our seats and the young girl who was interviewing us smiles from where she sits opposite.

"Hi, I'm Meghan, welcome to our show!" She has big bouncy blonde curls and a sweet smile that matched her bubbly energy and I feel bad that I was so tired and distracted. "How are you enjoying the city so far?"

"I wish we had more time to explore, honestly," Harper says with an equally sweet smile. "We're going to such cool places but we're only here for such a short amount of time. It's hard to get to see everything, or really anything, when we're working like this."

"That's unfortunate, is there anything you have been able to see since you've been here?"

"Not yet," Harper replies, "we just got in roughly an hour ago. Maybe we'll get to do some exploring after our show tonight." She's trying to sound optimistic, but I think we all know we're just going straight to the hotel after the show and unless I'm writing with Finn tonight, I'm going straight to bed.

"Hopefully you get to see some fun stuff tonight. I'll give you some recommendations after we're done if you'd like. But you as a band seemed to blow up overnight and it just seemed like, at least from my perspective, that you had your viral moment with your single Cosmic and then from there the EP came out and now you're on tour four months later. How has it been?"

"I think I can speak for everyone when I say it's been wild and overwhelming. Like you said, it happened so fast, and I know personally couldn't even really process it fully because we were in the thick of our senior year of high school and I was taking a bunch of AP classes and trying to keep my grades up is overwhelming enough on its own," Aspen says with a warm smile.

"I don't think it's actually set in yet, to be completely honest," Mari adds. "It's still wild that we're here doing this every night and getting to make such cool music. It's unreal."

"You've also gone viral for a rather unfortunate mishap during one of your shows last week. Can you tell me a little more about what happened there and what the response has been?" Meghan asks and we all look to each other and to Stevie for direction.

"We were really just having a rough day all around," Harper says, handling the question like a pro. "We blew a tire on our way from the last city and then we ended up on the side of the road for hours waiting for roadside assistance, so we didn't really have much time to prep before the show was scheduled to start. So we weren't able to have much of a soundcheck and we, had issues during the start of the show. But I'm pretty proud of us for how we handled it. We couldn't really hear ourselves which makes performing really hard, but we've known each other for so long that silent communication just flows so nicely, and we were able to work around it until we were able to hear ourselves again."

"I think that's one of the really great things about being childhood friends. We all know each other so well that when we had an issue, we were able to pick up on it and then were able to work together to work around it in a really organic way, I think. But those videos are awful," Finn smiles.

"I do think at one point during the show we apologized for technical issues and the crowd was amazing and so understanding. From what I've seen on social media, the general consensus has been about how resilient we are and how even after such a short time in this industry we're still so professional and handled ourselves so well. And I do think that's something we should be proud of." I smile. We really just did what we had to and hope it works out. We got lucky that it did.

"Now Kyle, I have to ask, as the resident heartthrob of the undead stars, I need to ask the question on everyone's lips. Are you dating anyone? And if not, do you have your eyes set on any specific person?"

I feel myself blush as I sit there, heat rising to my cheeks. How am I supposed to answer that? I can't just say that I'm crushing on our drummer. At least not publicly. "I guess I do have a crush on someone at the moment," I started speaking, not entirely sure where I was going, "but I am currently single." I let out a breath as Meghan seems satisfied with my answer.

"And don't forget that Kyle over there is like the gayest person I know," Mari says unprompted, causing Meghan to let out a startled laugh. I don't think anyone was really expecting that, and honestly, I'm not sure how I feel about Mari stating that fact. Not because I'm uncomfortable coming out to our audience or whatever, but there was something in the fact that I wasn't the one to do it. This interview will be public for the world to see and would be the first time my queerness is mentioned in the context of the band.

I look down at my hands where I've been absentmindedly picking off my nail polish the whole time we've been sitting here.

The conversation swiftly changed focus to what's coming next for us as a band.

Harper smiles and answered eloquently stating that though we are all going our separate ways for school, we are planning to continue working and creating as a band using school breaks and whatever time we can find to spend working together. She mentions the album, which is of course exciting though there's not much we can really say.

Though I've completely checked out of the conversation. It's not intentional at all. And I do feel bad for it. But this interview is going to be public in roughly a week, and at that point people are going to see it, obviously. And it's not like I have anything against being out publicly. I actually don't see a problem with it. But I can hear what my dad's going to say in the back of my head. I just know if I was home, I'd be grounded for that and it's not even something I said, but it's still being put out there.

After a few more follow-up questions about the album and the visions we have for the future, Meghan wraps up the interview and left the five of us in the room with Stevie to debrief.

Stevie is standing in the same spot, stone-faced as she had been the whole interview and it's making me nervous as we sit and wait for her comments. Not that I thought she'd have anything negative to say, but she has been wanting to work on our image and how we are perceived by the world as a band and I can't blame her. It's incredibly important, but the way she's just staring at us in silence has me on edge. If she has any inkling that my comment about having a crush was about Finn, that could cause a problem for me.

"You all handled yourselves very well," Stevie says as a smile starts to slowly spread across her face. "Very professional. Though I do have one comment." I hold my breath as I wait for what she's going to say. "Just like when you're on stage, when you walk into an interview, whatever's happening around you doesn't matter. You are to be focused. You are to be engaged. You should not be staring off into the distance with your eyes glazed over thinking about God knows what. The interviewer's time is just as important as yours. Do not waste it."

I definitely felt called out and felt myself blushing. She gave us a fifteen-minute warning before sending us off to do whatever we needed to before the show.

I get back to our dressing room before Finn, who stayed back to talk to Mari about something. Sitting on the table is a folded piece of paper with Finn's name on it in Stevie's unmistakably sloppy cursive. I can't help myself. I open it.

Finnley,

You're mad at me, and I get it. I'd be mad at me, too. What I said to you was awful. I was stressed and in the heat of the moment I said a bunch of things I know I shouldn't have. I was looking for someone to blame so I didn't have to blame myself, and I know so much of that is so very wrong. I shouldn't have let my frustrations get the

better of me. You deserve to be treated better. You've been ignoring my texts, and I understand I wouldn't want to answer me either, but I do think we should at least talk and talk this out. I still love you deeply and I'm not ready for this to be over. I care for you, and for this job and I guess I put that in jeopardy the second I kissed you six months ago, but I couldn't continue to deny those feelings. Still being here with you like this... I just miss you. I want to work things out if you can find it in your heart to forgive me.
Love you always,
S

I stare at the letter in my hands and want nothing more than to just crumple it up and throw it out. I want to toss it in the trash and make sure Finn never sees it. It's not like they're going to be alone in a room with Stevie anytime soon. Plus, she clearly cares more about her job than she does about Finn and their relationship. If I keep this from them, I'm actually helping them. They don't need to know about this at all. If they read this, it'll only hurt them more and they are working so hard to get over Stevie and get to a place where they're okay again.

I tuck the note away in my back pocket right as Finn walks in.

Chapter Nine

The next day is our first in the studio as a band. We've been making steady progress on the song we played on the side of the road, and Stevie found us a studio that we could book for a few hours to record some of it.

The studio is a small and cramped space with wooden floors and a rug covering the majority of the floor in a dark red that matched the color of the walls.

Chairs are pulled out and moved about the room, but I chose to sit on the floor with my guitar in my lap and just mess around. While everyone was talking and trying to discuss concepts I kept playing with the chord progression, changing little things up and adding variety to what I was playing. We had come up with a general idea for what we had wanted the song to sound like when we were on the side of the road, but it was very bare bones and there was plenty of room to work up to something we all really loved.

Harper is sitting with her notebook out in front of her,

writing out lyrics.. The song is really hers. She had come up with this idea during a sleepover with Aspen and had spent a while that night trying to perfect it until Aspen threw a pillow at her to shut her up.

So now she was back to writing but she kept saying there were some words that just didn't fit right. I could hear what she was saying, sure, but I'm not all that good with words so I left it to the others to help there. What I did feel I was pretty good at, though, was the musicality of the song and everything that was going on in the background, so that's where I focused my energy.

After about twenty minutes of us fiddling around separately, Finn came over to sit on the floor next to me.

"Hey," I say softly, almost like a whisper.

"Hey," they reply before gesturing at me to continue playing. "I really like how those sound, but maybe try it like this. May I?" They had this really hopeful and excited look on their face and how could I have forgotten they used to play guitar? I slowly pass my guitar to them, watching as they play exactly what I had played before, but changing the riff slightly.

There was something so beautiful about watching them playing my guitar. The way their hands move across the fretboard and how gentle they are with the strings. It's mesmerizing.

I didn't even notice when the entire room went silent. Everyone was fully enraptured watching them play. Listening to the delicate way they played each chord. It was so different from the fervor that I played with. The intensity I was using seemed so jarring in comparison.

Finn looked rather shocked and a bit uneasy as they looked up to see the entire room staring at them. The blush that spread across their cheeks was cute to say the least. They were completely and utterly flustered by the attention.

"I was just helping Kyle with the chord progression he's working on. We can mess around a bit more with it to match the tone and vibe of what y'all are writing, but I just kind of had an idea." Finn handed my guitar back to me and got up to head back over to the drums. Looking almost embarrassed. Though I'm not sure why. What they had played was amazing. It was perfect, really. Exactly what we needed.

"I really like what you were showing me. You play really beautifully, you know, maybe you could teach me how to be so gentle." I meant that in the sweetest and kindest way possible, but with this group I just had to pray that my words were being taken seriously. And maybe, just maybe, I was trying to flirt a little.

"Kyle, you need someone to teach you how to be gentle in general, guitar or not," Mari says with a laugh. "I know you mean well, but you're always so aggressive."

Now it was my turn to blush. This group hasn't really ever seen my softer side. The side of me that sits with Aubrey for hours during a panic attack or talks her off the brink of one. They don't often see that version of myself. The only person that has is Aspen, and even then we've barely scratched the surface there.

"I can be gentle when I want to be."

"Oh yeah? You should take that as a challenge." Mari smirks. "With what we've been writing over on this side of the room, I think that's what the song needs."

I nod and pull my guitar into my lap and try to play it just as Finn had. It doesn't sound as good, that I'm sure of, but it sounds pretty close. It's just something for me to work on. Something for Finn and me to work on.

I play through it a couple of times, referencing what I had written down, and then Aspen and Mari got up to join in.. Finn starts with a slow beat, and then Harper comes in with the lyrics she had been working on with Aspen and Mari.

What we were playing was far from perfect. Anyone could see that. But it had potential. Good bones. A good structure to go off of.. We had the potential to be something great.

We were just getting to the point where we were starting to have things written down. Starting to iron out the kinks. Starting to tinker and toy with the song, the words, the chords, the vibe we wanted to produce. It might take a while for it to become something that would be perfect. Something that we would be willing to put out, but we were on the right track.

The collaborative effort between all of us was something I was feeling really good about. Were we about to write a whole album like this? Were we finally working together in a way that felt true to who we are and true to each other?

But just as we were getting deep into the zone with the song, and really working collaboratively on it in a nice and organic way, Stevie came in to interrupt us. We had to head to the venue for that evening's show. We'd have to come back to this later.

♬

I sat watching Finn put on their makeup. They had a

rather large assortment of tubes and bottles laid out in front of them. Everything they had lined up perfectly and I watched them, mesmerized at how they just transform their face. They always look so cool when they are wearing makeup, especially like this.

I watch as they add different elements step by step until their makeup is complete, and they just look absolutely amazing.

They turn to look at me in my half-dressed state and catch me staring. Like any normal person would, I immediately avert my eyes, but I can't help the blush that's creeping up my cheeks.

"Like what you see?" They ask in that teasing tone I love so much and holy shit how am I supposed to respond to that?

I clear my throat, looking up at them and meeting their gaze. "Uh, yeah. I mean, you look good. You always do." I look at their eyes and notice that they've done their eyeliner differently than normal. It's all smudgy around their eyes and makes them really pop. God their eyes are beautiful. "You did something different with the, uh, the eyes. It's all dark and cool looking. I like it," I say tripping over my words.

"I can do some on you, if you want," they suggest and I know I would absolutely love that. I've always wanted to try makeup. But I've also always known that it was just something I would never do. My dad would actually murder me if he saw me with makeup on.

"I shouldn't," I say with a sad sigh, if I could I'd let them do it in a heartbeat, but I know for a fact that I can never be caught wearing even a tinted lip balm before my dad is going to call me screaming. "Besides, we probably don't have enough time to do it."

"We have plenty of time, if you really want to, but I'm not going to pressure you to do it. You've just always talked about how much you've wanted to try it, and your dad's not here to stop you. You can't let him keep controlling you. If you don't want to, I'll put everything away." They look at me, soft and sweet, and everything in me is screaming to say yes. Before I even realize it, I'm nodding, and they light up as they shove me into a nearby chair.

"Just close your eyes and let me do the rest," they say softly and I put all of my trust into them, closing my eyes.

I first feel something slightly cold on my eyelids. It's not their finger and it feels weird. Not wet exactly, but it's not like a powder either. And then they're using their finger and they're so gentle with me, their touch is so soft and feather light as they work on my eyes.

I then feel what I can only assume is the eyeliner pencil coming in contact with my lids. It's a weird sensation. It's almost like a kindergartener has taken a crayon to my eyelids. And then there's the brush. It's so soft and ticklish, I want to laugh but at the same time I don't want to disturb their work, so I hold myself together and let them continue to work on my eyelids.

"Okay, go ahead and open please," they say and I open my eyes and can feel a sheepish smile forming on my face. I just want them to think I look good. They smile at me and I melt.

They hold out a weird, sort of spiky looking brush and I eye it warily. "Okay princess, I'm going to do mascara now, just stay very still. I'll teach you how to do this another time so you can do it yourself, but for now I'm going to do my very best." They sound nervous and they gently tug on my eyelid and then bring the brush towards my open eye to put it on me.

They pull away from me once they're done with both eyes and smile. They have this proud look on their face, and they make a few adjustments.

"The only thing I think it's missing is glitter, if you want." I think about it for a second before shaking my head. The eyeliner is more than enough. I would love to be wearing glitter. How cool would it be to go onto stage with glitter on my face? The way it would reflect the lights on the stage would be insane. But I'm already going to be chewed out for the fact that I still haven't taken off the nail polish, and now I'm wearing eyeliner, and when the interview gets posted my dad's going to have a problem with that too. I can only handle so much. So, no glitter. It's the safer option. And maybe, somehow, there is a way that this isn't an issue, and my father would actually let me express myself however I want, let me explore what my style could be if I had the choice. Let me explore exactly who I want to be, and not be forced into this mold that he has shaped for me.

Finn nods and puts their makeup away quietly as I open my phone to take a look at the makeup. It looks good. So good. By the end of the summer, I'm going to learn how to do this myself. I'm going to learn how to put on makeup. And maybe I can convince my dad that it's just for the stage, and plenty of straight male musicians wear makeup onstage. This can be normal if I want it to be.

Chapter Ten

After the show, we go up to our room and I immediately flop down on one of the beds, effectively claiming it and just lay there for a minute before getting up to open my suitcase.

"I'm going to shower if that's cool with you," I said, simply trying to be polite, heading towards the bathroom as Finn let out a grunt of approval. I turn on the shower and let the warm water soothe me for a minute, cleaning myself as best I can before taking care of the obvious, washing my hair, body, and brushing my teeth and, for the very first time, attempting clean the black smudges off of my eyes that the eyeliner left behind.

I scrub at my eyes with whatever soap was in the bathroom and hope it's enough to remove the eyeliner and mascara, but it's stubborn and doesn't want to come off. Once I'm out of the shower I continue to scrub at my eyes with the rough towel, but it doesn't do much except spread the black all around my face. Somehow, I'm only making this worse.

After about twenty minutes I emerge from the bathroom, towel wrapped around my waist, looking like a raccoon. Clearly, I had no idea what I was doing. Taking off makeup was completely new to me.

"Wow that is just sad," Finn remarks after taking a minute to take in the poor attempt at a makeup removal job and laughing at me of course. "Here let me help you before you give yourself an eye infection." Finn gets up from where they were sitting on their bed with a book in their hands and grabs a makeup wipe from the pack they had left out on the dresser.

"Typically, I try to take off my makeup before I get in the shower, but I know plenty of people who like to do take most of their makeup off in the shower and then get whatever's left with a makeup wipe after." They carefully bring the cool wipe up to my eyes and gently remove the rest of the eyeliner smudges. My breath caught in my throat at the way they held my face still as they swiped the wipe under my eyes and across both my eyelids, and a bit on my left cheekbone, I have no idea how the makeup got there. There was truly something rather sensual about the way they held my face in their hand and I became hyper aware that I was practically nude straight out of the shower.

I try my best to keep my breathing steady as they worked, but I can't. They are just so soft and gentle with me and with my face in their hands all I want to do was kiss them or be kissed by them. All I can think about is kissing them, my eyes on their lips as they gently swipe the makeup wipe across my cheeks. With them so close I could count every freckle and as I look into their eyes, or try to, I can't help but stare at the small scar above their left eyebrow. I can just imagine kissing them there all sweet. But I know I can't. They're my friend, my bandmate, we work together. And not to mention they just got out of a relationship with someone we work with. I should know better. I *do* know better. These thoughts will be nothing more than thoughts. They will stay here in the comfort of my brain, and no one has to know. No one will ever know.

"There," they say breathlessly, "you're all cleaned up." They pull back and go over to their own suitcase, grabbing their toiletries from the bag and then head into the bathroom to take their own turn showering. Leaving me alone in the room to change into my pajamas.

While they shower, I do what any sensible person in my position would do, put on my pajamas which really just consisted of a pair of sweatpants, and then climb into bed to scroll through my social media.

While I was in the shower, Stevie had sent over some of the photos from the show and of course I had to look through them. There was this one really great group shot of all of us on the stage with the lights forming a sort of starburst behind us. Harper stood front and center and with the way she put her hair up she looks so badass. Mari is directly next to Harper, with her blue hair peeking through and being picked up by the light, contrasted by Aspen on her other side with her light blonde hair and pink highlights. Aspen's wearing a really cute dress and just looks incredible. And then there's Finn on the other side of Harper. And though they're positioned behind us on the stage, the angle has them in between Harper and I as if we're in a line across the stage, when in actuality we're all staggered across the stage. It's just one of those moments when Finn's head is tilted back ever so slightly, and their eyes are closed and god they look gorgeous. In most of the pictures they're either looking down or looking to the side, rarely forward like this, and it just looks so good. And then at the very end there's me. I'm looking down with my hair flopping in my face and you can't even make out my face let alone my makeup. It's a perfect picture. It will be the first picture amongst the carousel I post later or tomorrow or whenever I get the chance. Maybe if I'm lucky my dad won't look through the rest and see all of the pictures of me with makeup on. Maybe I can get away with it.

"Are you just sleep shirtless or is this just for me?" Finn teases as they emerge from the bathroom in sweats that I didn't even notice them bring into the bathroom. I look up from my phone and smile at them.

"Oh, I'm most certainly doing this just for you," I tease back, finding comfort in our usual banter. "Just be glad I'm wearing sweatpants, I normally sleep fully in the nude." I smirk at them and when they chuckle, I can't help but melt the tiniest bit.

"Well in that case, thank you for your service in covering up just for me. I greatly appreciate it." They smile at me playfully. This is flirting, right? We are flirting now, right? If it was anyone else, I'd think they were flirting so by that logic, Finn and I are flirting. But this has also just been how we've always talked to each other. So, what does that mean?

"It's my pleasure. I wouldn't want to subject you to anything that might make you uncomfortable."

They smile at me, and I can't help my gaze going right

back to their lips and I swear their eyes linger on mine for a second.

"How very kind of you. I, on the other hand, strive to make you incredibly uncomfortable." Finn laughs.

"Ah yes, because sleeping fully clothed will only serve to make me uncomfortable." I use this as an excuse to look them up and down and even in the sweats they're so beautiful.

"To each their own, as long as you're uncomfortable I'm happy."

"Well then we should keep it that way," I couldn't help but smile lying back on my bed. "I wouldn't want to make you unhappy."

Finn chuckles and then gets up and turned the lights off before getting in their own bed. "Goodnight, princess."

The next day is our first day off. Or it was supposed to be. It's not really much of a day off now though, it's a recording day, and a major one at that. We're getting back into the studio to record the song that we've been working on and while others are in the booth recording, we're starting to be grouped off to work on a few different ideas at once. It's how Stevie thinks we're going to get this album done in a timely manner, and we can only hope that it's going to work.

For today's writing session, I will be brainstorming and working on ideas with Harper. Honestly, I'm both excited and nervous to be working with her. We're just not super close, which has never really been an issue. We've worked fine in group settings, but the two of us don't really spend time together one on one. We don't really have conversations outside of the group conversations. So, while I know for the most part what's going on with her and what she's going through because we all talk to each other, sometimes it feels like I don't really know her. And that's not to say I don't love her, I do. I love her just like I love the rest of the band. But writing together might be tricky. At least at first.

We sit in a small room together. Me with my guitar on my lap and a notebook laid out in front of me, and her by the small keyboard in the corner of the room with her notebook in front of her. We both looked at each other, not really sure where to start. How do we go and bear our souls to each other when we feel like we don't really know each other? How do we just get super close to each other in such a short period of time. How do we make this happen quickly?

"So," I said after a few minutes trying to fill the empty space in some way shape or form. "Do you have any ideas?" If we could just find a place to start, then we could figure the rest out. And it's not like writing about my massive crush on Finn with Harper who doesn't really know me all that well is going to be the way to go.

"I don't really know," she says with a sigh. "I have a few ideas I guess, but they're just all really personal." She looks down at her lap as she speaks, clearly avoiding eye contact.

"Is there any you feel like sharing or do you want to just start fresh and brainstorm a completely new idea?" I ask trying to be a good friend and be on her side as best as I can while not overstepping this line that she's clearly not willing to cross with me yet.

"I guess, there's one I've been sort of tinkering with about an unrequited love in a weird sort of way. I really only have one verse right now, if that's cool with you," she says hesitantly, only looking up at me when she's done speaking as if looking for my approval.

"I'd love to hear it." I smile hoping to ease her nerves and excited to hear whatever she's wanting to play for me.

I expect Harper to pull her phone out and play me a voice memo, but what she does is move her notebook off the keyboard and close her eyes and she plays a few basic chords under the lyrics she's written. She has a very strong framework in the singular verse that she's written and the description in the verse is just so beautiful. I've always admired Harper's writing, but this is unlike anything she's written before. It's breathtaking. And I'm honored to be asked to work on it with her.

She finishes playing and pulls her hands away from the keys, slowly opening her eyes to search mine. "What do you think?" she asks and she looks so scared and timid. I've never seen her so nervous to share something. The normal confidence I'm used to is nowhere to be found. This song clearly means the world to her.

"That was really beautiful," I say after a few seconds, once I find my voice again. "You really want me to work on it with you?"

"I know you won't judge me like they will," she replies and it stops me in my tracks. I'd never judge anyone, that I know. But I've never felt like any of our bandmates would either. Especially not another member of the band.

"What do you mean?" I ask cautiously, trying to be mindful of not overstepping.

"Well, it just has to do with who it's about. I just," she sighs and tries to collect her thoughts, playing with her hair nervously. "I just can't tell them."

"Why not?" What have I done, or haven't done, that

has made her feel so comfortable with me. Not that I think it's a bad thing, but it's just not what I was expecting. Not from Harper. "He sounds like a really great guy. Wouldn't they just be happy for you."

"That's the thing." She looks back towards her lap fidgeting with her hands, refusing to look up at me. "It's not about a guy. It's about a girl."

"Oh," I say softly, placing my guitar down and getting up and crossing the room to go sit next to her on the bench in front of the keyboard. "And you're not ready to tell them yet?" I ask tentatively.

"I guess. I don't know. I just, I haven't told anyone else yet. I've barely even said it out loud. It's just so scary." I look at Harper and see the tears in her eyes and so I do what any reasonable person in this situation would do. I wrap her in a big hug and hold her while she cries. I've been where she is. I know it's scary. But I also know she'll be okay.

"I know it's scary, and I know it feels like everything is changing. And I know the scariest part is that you are going to lose people who mean the world to you. I've been there. It's not fun. But you will be okay. There is nothing you can do to change this part of you, the only thing you can do is learn to embrace and love this side of you. And we can write song after song about all of these scary feelings until it feels okay. I can promise you that. I know exactly what you're going through, I'm still fucking going through it, and it's not easy, but you are not alone." I feel like I'm speaking out of my ass saying all of the cheesiest things I can think of, but I only hope it can help.

She nods and pulls back from me, wiping her tears. "But how do we write about it without telling everyone else?" I can see it in her face her mind is racing a million miles a minute even as she's trying to calm herself down.

"If anyone asks, you were helping me work through some of my own shit through songwriting. But I don't think they'll read too much into it. But we can keep writing this song if you want to. Just keep writing it as we have it now. If that works for you."

"Sounds great." She smiles at me, and I can't help but feel like I've won. I've done the thing. I've been the good friend. I've been the friend she needed. And now there's this newfound friendship between the two of us. And it's new and we're still navigating it but spending time and working with Harper is going to be fun. I just know it.

We spend the next few hours working on the song together. Or at least we're working on what we think is one song. We're using the verse she had written as a baseline for the rest of the song. We're able to build it up and move through the song until we get to the bridge. It's only as we finish the bridge, we realize we've been writing a completely different song. Yes, we've been writing about having a crush and this unrequited love, but it's not just about her crush anymore. It's deeper than that.

All of a sudden, we put a pause on that song and start working on this other song that we seem to have written into the bridge. We pull the bridge out, toy with the melody and this song feels deeper. We keep messing with it, playing with different phrases and different words until what was a bridge has been turned into this sad, melancholic chorus about learning to be yourself and love yourself.

By the time Harper is pulled out of the session to go record vocals for the song that we as a band had finished, we're sitting with two half-finished songs that are almost ready to be brought to the rest of the band. And it feels good.

Once Harper's finished recording her vocals Stevie is rushing us out of the studio. She's scheduled for us to have a photoshoot for a magazine. Before we were working on the album this would have been the only thing we would have been doing today, but with the album having to take priority to literally everything else that we're doing, our days have just gotten way fuller.

The drive to the location for the shoot was about an hour away, so we loaded up the van and headed on our way.

Chapter Eleven

We arrived at the location for the shoot right on time, just as planned. There were ten to fifteen people all around setting up for the shoot, maybe more, and it was overwhelming. There were five of us, six if you count Stevie, yet it feels like there's nearly fifty people around to help us.

We were all pulled in different directions to get ready. There were stylists and makeup artists and an entire team of people around just to make sure we looked good. There were a handful of outfits for me to try on and I was immediately shoved into a dressing room. They had me trying on a few different pairs of jeans, some were different colors, others were different cuts, until they found the one they liked the best on me. The jeans they settled on were baggier than I was used to, and a little bit longer too, but a similar greyish-black color to what I've been wearing.

But since this shoot wasn't going to come out until the fall, they were dressing us in fall colors and fall attire, meaning for me they had a bunch of these really baggy sweaters in a variety of different dark colors. They pulled out my red and black guitar to compare with the outfit since there would be some shots with me holding it and nothing was working like they wanted, until they found and pulled out a sweater that was the same red as my guitar. It was on the thinner and lighter side, which I didn't mind at all, especially considering we were going to be shooting outside in the middle of the summer. The sweater was unlike anything I had worn before. Along with the black and red stripes there were a handful of rips and pulls throughout the fabric. It was perfectly my style in the best way.

The shoes were an easier pick. They just had me throw on a bunch of different and random pairs until they found ones they liked. But then it came time for jewelry and the stylist had a field day. The rings that I normally wear were pulled off and immediately replaced with new rings that were much nicer and higher quality. And they looked really cool. There were a lot of big, chunky rings that were put on me, and adjusted. Some were stacked, which was something I had never seen or even really thought of doing on my own. Then there was a watch thrown on my wrist. It's not my favorite thing. And maybe that's just because I don't wear watches often, but it just isn't really my vibe. But that's fine. They grabbed a few chunkier chain necklaces and put them on me, adjusting them as needed until it gave them the look they wanted. The stylist kept making comments about what she could do if I had pierced ears and, as cool as that would be, my dad would never let me in a million years. He would remove the earrings so fast and let the holes close before I have the chance to let them heal.

Once I was done getting styled and put into the outfit, jewelry, and all the other accessories, I was ushered into hair and makeup. My hair was immediately pulled back from my face with some clips as the makeup artist began to work.

It was weird, having someone put a full face of makeup on me. It was nowhere as intimate as what Finn had done the night before. She worked quickly and efficiently with a set makeup plan from whoever was in charge of the shoot. After last night, having makeup put on me felt familiar. I wasn't as jumpy as I probably would have been with all sorts of brushes and tools coming at my face.

While the makeup artist worked, someone else came over and started to paint my nails in a color similar to the black I had on previously. However, this time she added this sparkly powder thing over top to make them shimmery and really cool looking.

Once the makeup artist was finished applying my makeup, she hands me a mirror so I can take a look at it. It looks amazing. *I* look amazing. The eyeliner is all soft and smudgy like Finn had done the other day and there is this silver glitter all over my eyelids and cheeks. It's super subtle, but it looks so cool and makes my eyes look so green. I can't help but take a few selfies to send to Perri and Aubrey later.

And before I know it, I'm being ushered to the set.. As I get there, they are doing some solo shots of Aspen, who is looking so cool standing up there with her hair styled in a way that really brings out the pink highlights in her blonde hair.

I stand off to the side, watching as the photographers get the beautiful shots of Aspen, curiously looking for Finn to check out how they've been styled. They must look so amazing. I just can't wait to see how good they must look.

I'm standing off to the side waiting when I feel my phone start to buzz in my pocket. I curse silently. At some point I was supposed to give it to someone, I think. I'm pretty sure I'm not supposed to have it. I glance at the screen to see that my dad's calling me. Of course he is.

"Hey dad, can I call you back? Now's not really a good time," I say into the phone as I move to find an empty corner.

"You've been avoiding my calls. I think now is a pretty good time," he replies and I look back to where everyone else is and see Stevie glaring at me. Shit.

"I'm really busy. I'll call you tonight." I just need to get my dad off my back. Just for a minute. That's all I need, but he's insistent.

"We need to talk about what you were doing last night first."

I sigh audibly. Of course, he would call me to discuss what I had worn to the show last night. Especially considering I was wearing makeup.

"Dad, I'm working right now. I will call you later," I say again, but I know it's futile. I know I could just hang up and then I wouldn't have to worry about any of this, but I know that will just make him madder.

"What the hell were you thinking wearing makeup onstage like that? You looked ridiculous."

"I was just trying something different. I won't do it again." I know I'm lying through my teeth. I want to argue but I know it's not the time.

"And I thought you were going to take off that nail polish. Why do you still have it on?"

"I just haven't had the chance to take it off yet. I'll do it when I get the chance. I've been really busy, dad." I look over and see Stevie glaring at me and I try to shoot her an apologetic glance, but I doubt it'll matter. I'm in trouble.

"Just do it. And don't let me catch you wearing that makeup again. Understood?"

"Yes. Now I really have to go." I hang up before he can say anything else, and I just know I'm going to face his wrath for that later.

I walk back over to where I had been standing as Aspen finishes up and they pull Harper up to do her solo shots. I look around the room and there's still no sight of Finn. Should I be worried? Are they okay? Did something happen? I can't help but worry as the rest of us are all here, seemingly ready. However, I don't have much time to really worry about anything before I see Stevie marching over, her glare fixed on me.

Stevie grabs me by the arm and pulls me back towards the corner I had taken the phone call from my dad in. She stands there for a minute with her hand outstretched waiting for me to place my phone in it.

"What the hell was that?" she asks as soon as I hand her my phone.

"My dad called. He's been trying to call me all day," I say, knowing that it's no excuse, but I can only hope for it to help in this situation.

"Why the hell do you even have your phone with you? It was supposed to be left in your dressing room. Are you having a problem following basic instructions?"

"I just forgot. I didn't mean anything by it."

"Do you know how awful this looks for all of us? The

directions were simple yet you're here on set taking phone calls like you're better than the rest of it."

"It was an honest mistake. It won't happen again,"

"An honest mistake? Is that what I'm supposed to believe?"

"It's the truth." She fixes me with a stare that makes me think she doesn't believe me. "I have nothing to hide. I was ignoring my dad's calls when I was writing with Harper, and he just really needed to get in touch with me apparently."

"Apparently?"

"He was calling me over something stupid. I should have just ignored the call, but after that many calls I got worried something had happened." Now that was a straight up lie, not that she has to know. I knew exactly what my dad was calling me about. It was so insanely obvious after how I went out on stage last night.

"Fine. Don't let it happen again. Got it?"

"Yeah. It won't happen again." Stevie then releases me back out to the rest of the group, and I go and stand with Aspen and Mari as Harper continues to be photographed. Finn is still nowhere to be found, and now I'm really concerned. It's not like them to be late to anything. If anything, I'm the one that's always making the two of us late.

I look to the door where the rest of us had come in from and there they are, walking in with a nervous smile, and holy shit they look amazing. They're wearing a black lace top with a burgundy corset overtop, a pair of black pants, and these really pointy boots with a heel on them. And their makeup. It's like what they did with the black smudgy eyeliner, but make that the whole eye, and their lipstick is a burgundy shade that matches the corset perfectly. They look so hot. It's not like anything I've ever seen them wear before. It's not like anything I've seen anyone wear before.

They walk over to the rest of us and stand right next to me. How am I supposed to pay attention to the shoot and to what's going on around me when they're standing next to me looking like that?

"Hi," I whisper, trying to be quiet to keep from disturbing the peace as Harper and Mari switch out. I'm next. "You look really good." I look over to their face just for a second and I can see them blushing ever so slightly underneath all of the makeup that they have on.

"Thanks. So do you." They reply as their eyes rake over my body. I can't help but let mine do the same as I feel a blush start to creep up my own cheeks. We stare at each other for a while before I'm called to go up and have my solo shots taken. And I swear if we weren't at this shoot, or just in public like this I might not be able to control myself.

The shoot itself is somehow both scary and fun at the same time once I'm in it. On one hand, it feels like there's a million eyes on me and there's a bunch of people yelling at me and telling me what to do and it feels so overwhelming, but on the other, I can finally hear the music that has been playing on the speakers all day and it's ours, which is really cool. With my guitar in my hand, standing, sitting, and leaning on all the different set pieces just feels so cool and natural. I keep changing my positions as I'm told to until they're done with me. I can only hope that I'm looking good in at least a few of the shots, but they did all feel really good, and by the blush that has seemingly taken up residence on Finn's cheeks, I think I did a pretty good job.

Finn goes last as they had arrived last and watching them has my jaw on the floor. They just look so hot and the way that they follow the direction and make every complex stance and position just look effortless has me in awe of them. I can't look away. My heart is racing, I'm definitely sweating, this is all too much. I can't just get up and leave. Not now. All I can do is watch. Though it's not like I could take my eyes away if I tried. They are gorgeous.

"Dude, you're drooling," Mari whispers to me, causing me to jump. Was I really being that noticeable? "We all know you're into them, but you don't need to be so obvious about it." I sigh. I hadn't meant to be so open with my staring, but I can't look away.

I try to tear my eyes away, but it's impossible. They just look so insanely amazing up there. Why would I want to? They follow the directions they're given with ease. Moving smoothly between poses and looking sexy while doing it. There isn't a single bad angle. They look amazing no matter how ridiculous of a pose is wanted. I can't even blink, worrying that if I do I'll miss even a second.

Eventually it's time for all of us to get up on the stage and take the group shots. Now, I thought the group shots would have been easier than the individual shots. Like they would just need to put us together and then snap a few pics. Easy enough, right? Wrong. Not only are they placing each of us in a certain way throughout the set, but they also have to position each of us, and it's not like they can really do that all at once. It takes time to place and position all of us so it looks just right. And it takes a while.

If I had to guess I'd say we spent about half an hour just setting up to get one or two shots. And the entire afternoon goes on like that. Each and every shot feels agonizing in just how long it takes. By the time we're heading back to our dressing rooms to get out of everything we're all exhausted.

Finn and I walk into our dressing room and luckily, I'm leading. For the first time since we've arrived at the set we have a moment to be alone where we're not being whisked off to different places with different people. We walk in and I see another one of those letters with Finn's name written in Stevie's handwriting. It's sitting right next to where I was supposed to put my phone. I grab it off the table and shove it into my pocket before we head our separate ways to get changed back into our own clothes. I can't read it in front of them. I know that much. I will find a time to read it that's not when we're sitting right next to each other, or even in the same room. Luckily they're in they're in their own world on their phone and don't even notice.

As I tuck the letter away into the small backpack I brought with me to the shoot, I can't help but feel like I'm doing something wrong. Especially with them standing not even five feet from me. If I'm not careful, they could see what I'm doing. That's the problem. But if they were to read this letter from Stevie it could just end up ruining anything we may or may not have with each other. If they were to see any of this, it would just end up hurting them more. Hurting them because I'm hiding it from them, sure, but hurting them because they would probably end up going back to Stevie and we both know they don't deserve that. Hell, the whole world knows they don't deserve that, but that's not going to stop them from going back to her. It wouldn't be the first time, according to them. Apparently this wasn't even the first time she cheated. And she was just awful to them. We all saw it. She did a great job hiding it for six months, but as soon as tensions got high, we all saw what they've been dealing with in private and none of us were okay with it.

So, I hide the letter from them. It's in their best interest. Maybe I'll read it later. Maybe I won't. Whether I do or not isn't an issue. The only thing that matters is that they don't read it. This may be the only way I have a chance with them. Why should they even consider going back to Stevie when I'm right here? Clearly, I'm the better option. If I'm even an option.

After we change back into our own clothes, we head out towards the van to drive back to the hotel and go to bed ready for our long drive to our show tomorrow.

Chapter Twelve

When we get to the hotel room, I make my way into the bathroom to take a shower. Only, I stop in my tracks when I look in the mirror and see I still have makeup on. How did I forget? And didn't Finn say something about taking the makeup off before getting into the shower? I quickly pull out a makeup wipe and began to scrub at my eyes, but the glitter just seems to go everywhere. Is that supposed to happen? How am I going to get it off?

I poke my head out of the bathroom to find Finn sitting on their bed, the sheets from the notepad we had been writing our song on laid out in front of them with the notepad from this hotel on their lap as they scribble on it.

"Uh, hey, quick question. Is this what's supposed to happen when I try to take the glitter off?" I ask, gesturing to my face which seems to be covered in the stuff, hating that I'm interrupting them, but getting a bit excited to know we're going to be working on the song tonight.

"Oh. Wow. Look at you. How did you get glitter all

over your cheeks when it was only on your eyes?" They say with a smile and a bit of a laugh.

"I don't know." I sigh. "I was using the makeup wipe like you showed me and it just started spreading all of the sparkly bits. Like it took care of the color, but... Did I do something wrong?"

"Other than be far too aggressive with your eyes?" I shoot them a confused look. "Your eyes are all red. You were really scrubbing at them, huh?" They reach up and gently touch the area around my eyes.

"Is that not how I was supposed to do it?" I ask genuinely, but they just laugh at me.

"Oh Kyle, there is so much I need to teach you. We'll worry about that later, but right now let me show you one of my favorite tricks that my sister taught me when I was big in my makeup phase a few years ago." The reach into their makeup bag and pull out a roll of patterned tape. "Washi tape. It's relatively gentle on the skin and does the trick." They rip a small piece and then stick it to a spot on my cheek and carefully remove it, showing me the sticky side so I could see all the glitter that was now on the tape and not on my skin.

"You won't get all of it off this way, but you'll be able to get a fair bit of it off." They hand me the roll and gesture for me to try it myself. I gently tear off a small piece of tape and stick it to the spot just under my eye before carefully peeling it off. On the sticky side of the tape was some of the glitter I had managed to cover my entire face with. I do it again, and again, and again until I felt like I had truly made a dent in the insane amount of glitter that is all over my face.

I look over to Finn like a kid in a candy shop full of pride after doing the one thing they had taught me.

"Look at you, you're finally learning something." They smirk. "But, seriously though, I need to take you makeup shopping soon. Especially if you're enjoying it as much as I think you are, we should get you some of your own."

I freeze at the mention of getting me my own makeup. Of course I would love that. In a perfect world Perri would have taught me how to put on makeup ages ago. But this isn't a perfect world and if I go home with makeup in my bag my dad might actually kill me.

"Oh, I'm not sure about that," I say with a laugh, hoping to not draw attention to my own anxiety without coming off as rude.

Finn just nods in response and then heads into the bathroom to take a shower. As soon as I'm in the room alone I pull out the note Stevie had left them and decide to read it. There's a small part of me that knows I shouldn't be reading the letter. I know it's not mine to read, but I just can't help myself, I let my curiosity get the better of me.

Finn,

You're mad at me. I understand that. What I did to you was awful, but not acknowledging my last letter? That's just cruel. I want to make things right between us. I really do. But I can't do that if you give me a chance. If you want space, and want to keep things between us professional, just say that and I'll stop.

I know I'm not going to be able to fix everything. I've come to terms with that. What I said was awful and I deeply regret it. I should have known better. I'm supposed to be the adult here.

Just please talk to me. I can't keep going on like this, it's so hurtful. How can I make things right? Tell me what I need to do, and I will do it. I just want things to be okay again. You know I don't want any harm to come to this band, and I've been working with the five of you for so long, if you want anyone to be on your team it should be me.

All I'm asking for is a few minutes of your time. That's it. I hope you can find it in you to at least give me that.

Love you always,

S

I fold the letter back up and tuck it away knowing Stevie is getting on my last nerve. I get that she cares about this band and her job so deeply, we all do, but the way she's going about this is only going to hurt Finn. They need time. They will go to her when they're ready, but clearly, they're just not ready yet and the way she's trying to pressure them to speak to her is infuriating.

To take my mind off of the infuriating way Stevie is trying to get back with Finn when she really doesn't deserve them, I pick up the notepad on Finn's bed and start to look over what they've been writing for our song today. I read through what they had written, and then read it again, and again. The words they had written just held me in their grip. It wasn't for the song we were working on. It was something new. But maybe, it is about us.

Late nights all alone
Summer sun and telephones
In my darkest nights you held me close
I'd never want for you to go
Same dream, separate life
Wonder if I'm always trailing behind
Then I see that look in your eyes

"What are you doing?" Finn asks as they walk out of the bathroom in their sweats, their hair still damp from the shower.

"This isn't for our song," Is all I can manage to say as they're looking at me with this sad, disappointed look in their eyes.

"I'm not just writing with you," they say and I know they're not. We spent all morning writing with other people. Of course I'm not the only person they're writing with. That's the only way we're going to piece this album together. So why does it hurt to think they wrote those words with someone else?

"No, I know that. I just assumed you were working on our song." I stumble over my words trying to find some reason as to why I had been looking through their stuff.

"Do you want to work on our song tonight?" They ask and I know it's been a long day, and they just look so tired. I want to say yes, but they probably just want to go to bed.

"If you're up for it. I know it's been a long day. And if you're looking for someone to work on whatever this is, unless it's what you were working with Mari on today then I guess maybe I should stay out of it. I should probably just stay out of your stuff and sit over here." I walk back over to my bed, my cheeks bright red with embarrassment.

"This," they take the notepad from my hand, and I realize I've been holding it this whole time, "is just an idea I had, something I was messing around with. We could work on it, but maybe later. I do want to work on the song we're almost done with. I just feel like it's not saying what I want it to say, if that makes sense."

I sigh, both relieved and frustrated. I want to work on that new song Finn's toying with. The idea is brilliant. It seems so cool and fun, and I want to play around with it and find the melody and the rest of the song, it could be so special. But we've already been working on this one song together and I guess even though I thought we were getting close to a good place with it, and getting close to finishing it, it's just not what Finn wants or needs it to be.

"So, what are you trying to say then?" I ask genuinely. Maybe I'm misunderstanding what they wanted to say with this song, and that's on me. But maybe I can help them figure out what they are trying to say with the song and make it into the song they want it to be.

"I don't know. Maybe we should scrap it and just work on this new one instead. I don't know. I just wanted it to really encapsulate the highs and lows of my relationship with Stevie and it just feels like it's falling flat. Like it's not actually saying what I need it to say, if that makes sense."

"I think you might need to explain it a little more for me." I'm on the edge of understanding what they're trying to say, but I'm not quite there yet. I need just a little more of an explanation and I'll get it, I'm sure of it.

"Okay, so like, it just feels like a normal, stereotypical, relationship. And with Stevie, when things were good, they were really good. When things were good, when work was good, when she was happy, I was treated almost like God. She loved me and she wanted me, and she made it very known that she felt that way. But when things were bad, when she was stressed, when she was just in a bad mood, well, you saw how bad things could get. And I don't know if this song is really holding all of that."

"Okay, that makes so much more sense. What do you feel like the song is holding?"

"I feel like we just wrote a song about all of my flaws and insecurities and issues and it's just not what I wanted it to be. It's like we've written a song about the bad times, about those days when she would just hate my existence and my transness and everything I'm trying to be and me not feeling like I'm good enough in this relationship. It's just all the bad moments and none of the good."

"Do you think that's because the bad moments are outweighing the good?" I ask, trying my best not to pry.

"I don't know. Maybe. The good moments were just, so good, but also maybe in a toxic way."

"Well, we still haven't written the bridge. Maybe there's something there?. We can find a way to make it about how even the good times, the times she lifted you up and made you feel like you were on top of the world, were just as bad. Maybe we start the bridge with a good moment, a moment where you felt like things were really good, but looking back it was too good. Maybe something bad was always lurking around the corner."

"Lurking around the corner, I like that." They write the phrase down and my heart just soars knowing I've maybe contributed a lyric. "I guess it did kind of feel like that sometimes. Like I always knew the good moments weren't going to last forever. I knew things were going to get bad again eventually."

"That's got to be like, really hard to deal with. Feeling like nothing good lasts."

"Oh, I like that! Something something, lurking around the corner, nothing good lasts longer than an hour. No, nothing good lasts for more than an hour. Not when she's in the room." They're writing on a fresh sheet of paper feverishly. "It's just a few lines before that and then something after. I just don't know what yet."

I nod as I'm leaning forward keyed in. "Tell me about one of those moments when things were good and then it felt like the switch was flipped."

"Hold on. What about *nothing good lasts for more than an hour, flipped the switch, the monster's always lurking there right around the corner* and then that feed back into the chorus."

I watch them cross out what had already been written as they rewrite the lines that are going to be the end of the chorus with excitement. "That's good! Really good. You just took a few things I said and turned them into song lyrics. It's impressive."

"Is it? It's just how my brain works, I guess. But to go back to your question, I think that party I threw for our EP release is a pretty good example. From the moment she was hosting, and we were setting up and making everything look nice she couldn't get her hands off of me. She kept saying she was just so proud of me and how much I was accomplishing. And with all of our friends and families there she really turned on the charm. Just like she always had in front of y'all, but then the party ended, and we were left to clean up in her apartment and it was just the two of us. I can't even tell you what I did or didn't do. But she just wouldn't talk to me. I spent the whole evening trying to start a conversation and trying to find something to talk about, but she wasn't hearing it. She just gave me the silent treatment. Which I guess is one of the tamer of her bad moods, but even still, it was hurtful."

The recount their recollection of the night and I can't help but think back to my own experience of the night. Aubrey and Perri had come, they had even gotten Taylor to come which was honestly an accomplishment when it came to the amount of time she had been spending with her boyfriend. But no matter who was there, and there were some pretty cool people there, all I noticed was my parents weren't. My mom had promised they'd be there, but at some point, my dad must have convinced her that they shouldn't or couldn't go. I kept looking towards the door waiting for them to just be fashionably late, but they never came. And I vaguely remember seeing Finn and Stevie together and seeing her all over them, but I most likely was just trying to avoid the both of them. I never really loved the way they were always all over each other in public.

"I remember her being kind of all over you that night. At least from what I saw. But I didn't see too much of you," I say, trying my best to offer my own perspective while not airing out my own issues from that night.

"We did spend a lot of time in her bedroom during the party. She was enjoying keeping me pretty hidden from everyone else who was there."

"Hidden?"

"She always wanted me all to herself. That was kind of always her thing. I was hers in a sense and so she didn't want me hanging around with other people who could get the wrong idea."

"That's really possessive."

"Yeah, I guess it is. She would just show me she loved me and make me feel so special."

"Make you feel like you were her whole world. The only thing that mattered."

"You're really good at writing these lyrics, Kyle." They start scribbling something down and I can only assume it's coming from something that I said.

"Showed me you loved me, but you held me too close, in broad daylight told me I was your world, but nothing good lasts for more than an hour, flipped the switch, the monster's always lurking there right around the corner." They look at me with triumph in their eyes as they finish writing the lyrics to what we think is going to be the bridge. And they're just so excited it's making me want to keep working.

We spend another hour messing with the chords and

the melody for the bridge until we find something that fits absolutely perfectly. Finn records it on their phone in their voice memos, eager to play it for the band in the car tomorrow as we drive to the next stop of our national tour. And I'm excited too. We worked on this together, and we worked hard, and now we get to share it with everyone. Who wouldn't be proud?

Chapter Thirteen

In the van the next morning, while we were all still half asleep, Finn plugged their phone into the aux and played the song we had spent most of the night working on. It was early, and no one wanted to be working at nearly six in the morning as we embarked on the long drive to the next city, but everyone listened anyway, ready to give feedback.

"It's good," is the first thing Harper says as the song comes to an end. She sounds hesitant and I can't help but worry that the rest of that sentence isn't going to be what we might want to hear.

Everyone else agrees, besides Stevie who is oddly quiet, perhaps catching on to the topic of the song.

"You don't sound too sure of that," Finn says, and I can hear a hint of hurt in their voice and it breaks my heart. I know how hard it was for them to write this song. Sure, I helped, but it's really their song. They worked so hard to make sure the song was getting across the message they wanted it too. They spent countless hours over the last few weeks pouring over the words on the page until they felt it was absolutely perfect. I want to reach over and grab their hand and squeeze it and show them that they're not alone in this, but I know I can't do that.

"I just," she sighs. I turn and look back at her and I can see how unsure she looks, staring down at her lap and picking at her cuticles. Whatever she's about to say has got to be hard for her. "It's a great song. It's beautiful, really. I just can't be the one to sing that. It's too personal." Mari and Aspen nod along to what Harper's saying and my heart aches for Finn. Putting all of that into words was a huge step for them. Even just playing that for everyone was confiding in all of us a truly deep feeling, a secret almost, something they weren't going to share with us. Something they almost didn't share with us. But they did, they put their trust in everyone in this car.

"All of our songs are personal. That's the whole point of songwriting, putting our feelings into songs. You've sung about everyone else's issues. You've sang songs that hold the hurt and pain of almost everyone else, but you're drawing the line at mine? You even sang that one song Kyle wrote for his best friend's dead sister, but my song is where you draw the line?" Finn sounds so calm, but the death grip they've got on the steering wheel says otherwise. Harper's crossing a line.

"We never did anything with Kyle's song." Harper tries to defend herself, but it's not making it any better. Sure, I had written a song for Aubrey to celebrate her sister, and I guess it was different, but saying it's different because we've never recorded it and put it out isn't what makes it different. In this case, it's no different than her singing a song that Finn wrote about his relationship with Stevie.

"So that makes it better? How is that supposed to make me feel better?"

"Dude, first of all, it's just a song you don't need to get so butthurt about it. And second, we all know this is about Stevie and I'm just not comfortable going up onstage and singing this song about our manager."

"You know damn well it's not 'just a song' and are you really going to sit here and defend Stevie after the way she was talking to them? Are you really going to take her side?" I say jumping to Finn's defense. After the way Harper and I worked to write our songs together and pour our deepest emotions and secrets into the lyrics the other day she should know what it means for them to have put all of this into a song, a package wrapped up with a pretty little bow, to put out into the world.

"Why are there sides?" Harper asks incredulously.

"What the fuck do you mean by that? You heard how Stevie was talking to them right? You heard how awful she was, right? And you're going to defend her by not being comfortable singing a song about the downfall of the relationship?"

"I just think the song is a little cruel. It completely glosses over most of what we've seen of their relationship."

"What we saw was barely a fraction of what that relationship looked like. And even if the song glosses over what you seem to think is the most important parts of the relationship, you don't get to decide what the most important parts were. You don't get to decide what caused pain and what was okay."

"I just think it will bring up more questions than we're willing to address."

"What do you mean by questions?" Finn asks and I can see in their eyes they're actually thinking it over, trying to understand where she might be coming from with this.

"Do you really want to have to spend the next however many years explaining your relationship with our manager?"

"Why would I have to do that? Why would that even have to be public knowledge? We both know that we all can talk about the song and what it means without bringing up who I was dating. That doesn't have to be a focal point at all. And sure Stevie's our manager but we can't forget she's also Mari's cousin."

"But it could come up."

"Only if you say something because I think the rest of us can agree that we don't need to make that public. I'm sure Stevie wants to keep it private just as much as I want to. But if you're so set on making it public, we can put the song off to the side and come back to it when we're all more awake and ready to discuss."

"So, I'm only opposing the song because I'm tired?"

"I never said that."

"Really? Because it really sounds like that's what you were trying to say."

"What I was trying to say is that I think we need to take a break from this conversation before we start saying things we don't mean."

"But I feel like I'm making a pretty valid point. You've written the relationship to be horrible and think you can get away with just avoiding talking about it? You can't be serious. The song is beautiful and gut wrenching and it's going to be a song people want to talk about. I don't see how you are going to be able to avoid it."

"I'm not the only person who's had an experience like this. The song could help so many people just feel seen. Isn't that the whole point of music? If we're not writing music to connect with others, what are we writing for?"

"You can connect with people without throwing Stevie under the bus. Especially with this. You've completely dramatized the whole thing."

"I get that we were all friends first, and you want to defend Stevie, but we don't even have to say a single thing about the song being about her. We don't have to name names. It's not like the relationship was ever super public."

"Hey why don't we just put the song to the side and come back to it if we need something to fill a slot or something. It doesn't have to make the final cut." They look and sound so defeated, and I just want to wrap them up in a big hug. It would be one thing for Harper, or anyone for that matter, to want to just tweak a few things and rework parts of the song to fit her as the singer, but to just flat out say no because of the subject matter isn't something I was expecting. Harper is usually all for calling someone out when they do something awful, why doesn't Stevie get that treatment?

After a few hours we stop at rest stop to get gas, grab lunch and snacks, and use the bathroom. While everyone gets out of the van and heads inside to get food and whatever else they might want, I hang back by the van with Finn.

"Are you okay?" I ask once I'm sure we're as alone as we're going to be standing outside the gas station.

They perk up and smile at me, but it feels forced. "Why wouldn't I be?"

"What Harper said… that wasn't okay. You don't deserve to be treated like that."

"It's just a song." They look down towards the cracked pavement and kick a rock across the parking lot.

"It's not just a song and I think we both know that."

"It's really not that big of a deal."

"It was last night."

"Well, that was last night. Right now, it's not that big of a deal. Right now, it's just a song."

"Bullshit. I know we all put little pieces of ourselves into the songs we write, but with that song, you put every single thought and feeling you've had about the relationship into it. You wrote exactly how you've been feeling, only for Harper to go and say it's just a song and one she's not comfortable singing because of the way it paints Stevie and how you might have to talk about the relationship in interviews and talk about how you were with her."

"The relationship was messy. Talking about it is messy. It is what it is. You don't need to make it a big deal. I'm over it."

"Finn, you can be honest with me. I know that song meant a lot to you. You worked so hard on it. Don't you want it to be part of the album?"

"I do, but it's just a song, and it was yours too. You did practically write the bridge last night."

"I just helped, kind of. It really was all you. And it was so hard for you to write because of how close you are to it all. Harper's opinion doesn't take away from that."

"Look, we might come back to the song. We might not. Every time we bring a song to the girls there's a chance they'll not want to use it for whatever reason. And Harper is the lead singer, it is kind of up to her as to whether or not she's comfortable singing something. And she's just not comfortable singing this. It's fine."

"But it's not fine. The song it—"

"Kyle, it's fine. Can you please just drop it? We'll talk about it later, okay?"

I want to keep arguing with them. I want to grab them by the shoulders and shake them and scream at them and allow them to feel however they really feel about this. But I know they're not going to let me in, not right now, anyways. We don't have much time anyways. The girls are walking back towards the van, and we have to keep on going.

"Maybe we can at least try and work on that other song you were working on last night?" I suggest. I don't know if it's a good idea. I doubt it is, in actuality. But to have a song that we've written together, something that maybe has a hint of how we feel about each other written into its very fabric might actually be what the band is looking for music wise, if they even feel the same way about me. But that song they were writing, those lyrics. That small section. It's not nothing. And I know working on it while I was just in the other room means nothing. It's probably not even about me. But what if it is?

"You know, princess, that idea isn't half bad. Maybe tonight we'll get working on that." They say and I swear I see them light up and look almost hopeful. Maybe I am onto something.

♫

Before the show that night Finn laid out all of their makeup as they normally would when getting ready. Everything was in a neat little line and ready for use. I was just staring at myself in the mirror, messing with my hair trying to keep it from sticking up in twelve different directions when Finn calls me over.

"Hey princess, can you come here for a second? I want to try something." They smile in that way that tells me it's going to be way more than a second, but they're still hoping to get me on board.

I smile warmly as I walk across the small dressing room over to where they're sitting.

"Come sit." They direct and I look across the table they've overrun with makeup for a random sheet of paper with song lyrics or really anything to work on, but don't find a single one.

"I don't bite. Normally." They tease as they see me looking around skeptically before taking a seat.

"I'm not sure I want to test that, yet." I tease back with a smirk.

"Okay, smartass. I was thinking I could teach you how to put on some basic makeup, so I don't have to keep doing it for you before every show. And maybe when we have a day off, or even an hour of free time, I'll take you shopping for some makeup." They look timidly excited and hopeful, and I just can't say no.

But I should say no, right? It's one thing to be wearing makeup at photo shoots or onstage, but learning how to apply the makeup, knowing what I'm doing and what others are doing when it comes to makeup. Isn't that just too far? Doing this is just going to make my dad angrier. Is that what I really want? Shouldn't I be trying to keep the peace?

I know I shouldn't be trying to aggravate him further, but I can't help but want to do something for myself. So, I sit down next to Finn and agree to let them teach me how to put on makeup. It's not like my dad ever has to know whether or not I can put on makeup. It's not like I'm walking into the house with bags and bags of makeup that I have bought. I'm just learning how to do something that I think I'm trying to make part of my "brand" anyway. It's not hurting anyone.

I look at all of the different packages and things that are all over this table in a messy but organized line. Am I going to be using all of this? Do I even need all of this?

"Okay, you're only going to be using about half of this. We're just going to keep our focus to your eyes as we have been. There's no need to worry about face makeup right now. I'm not even the same shade as you so that probably wouldn't end well. So, you're only going to need to use these. That's it."

They grab maybe five different items out of the lineup of close to twenty and put them in front of me. "Can we also do that sparkly stuff they did on my cheeks for the shoot? I really liked how that looked," I ask somewhat timidly. I know Finn has a whole plan as to how they're going to teach me and what this probably should look like and I don't want to step on their toes and start trying to do something completely different, but I also want to maybe expand what we're doing a little bit. If that's okay.

"Of course," they say with a smile and grab one more item from their lineup and put it in front of me. "We're going to start simple here." They pick up a small tube.

"I'm just going to have you follow what I'm doing on my own face, if you think you can do that. Do you think you can do that?"

I nod as I face them watching what they do intently. I can do whatever they need me to.

"Okay so we're going to start here," they pick up a small tube and begin to unscrew the top. "This is an eyeshadow primer. It's going to make everything we're putting on last all night and keep it in place. You don't need a lot of it. A little bit goes a long way." They pull the top up and then use the long thing that's attached to the cap to put a little bit on each eyelid. "Just put a little on and then blend it out with a finger."

They hand me the tube and I try to do the same thing. I pull the top out and try to just put a little bit on each eyelid. I then rub it in with my fingers just like they did.

"Okay, now we're going to add a little bit of glitter if you want. I know I want to wear some glitter, we can skip this if you don't want to, but the glitter did look really good on you the other day."

I feel my cheeks heat with a blush as they compliment me. I want to wear glitter. I want to wear it so badly. But is glitter going to be pushing it too far?

"Yeah, let's do some glitter," I say before letting myself overthink it. They smile and grab another thing off of the table.

"So, this little pot is a liquid glitter eyeshadow. I find it really easy to apply both with a brush and with a finger. For right now, I don't want to complicate things with brushes so we're going to use our fingers. We don't need a lot of this. A little goes a long way."

"You keep saying that." I smile.

"I've only said it twice."

"Sure, but how many times are you going to say it."

"Anyway, back to the makeup, you're just going to want to pat a little bit all over your eyelids." They demonstrate and I watch very carefully before going in and doing it for myself.

I try to only get a small amount of the glitter on my finger, but I end up trying to use way more than I had intended. It seems to want to go everywhere. I start to get frustrated, but before I can really start to freak out Finn is there with a makeup wipe to try and clean me up.

"There you go. I should've warned you how messy this stuff could be." I chuckle lightly as they fix up my makeup. "Maybe we should stick to powders for you from now on. That would probably be easier to work with."

I nod as I look at what we're working with. The mess of glitter around my eyes has been cleaned up and I look more put together.

"So now we're going to do eyeliner," they say as they pick up the eyeliner pencil. "I know this looks scary, but it's going to be made really easy, we're going to do the smoky look you really like."

"Smoky?"

"I think you've been calling it smudgy, but we're going to teach you the proper terminology for all of this stuff." I watch as they demonstrate how to apply the eyeliner, informing me that I'm allowed to make it messy. "Now we're going to use a brush, do you think you can handle it?" They tease after I successfully apply the eyeliner to my lids.

"I don't know, I couldn't even handle the glitter. I can't make any promises." I joke as they demonstrate how to get the eyeliner to look smudgy—no, *smoky*, just how I like it. They hand me the brush as I do the same as before, then they move on to teaching me how to apply mascara.

I practically stab myself in the eye twice before I get it semi decently and they just come back with that makeup wipe to clean up the mess I've made of my face.

"Now we're going to go back to a powder since you clearly can't handle the cream or liquid products to do that glitter on your cheeks. That is called highlighter." They explain to me taking the tone they would use for a toddler, and I just nod along completely enraptured by them.

They hand me the product with a smile, and I look at it confused. "What am I supposed to do with this?"

"Well, I'm not on that step of my makeup process yet. So, either you're just going to go for it with me talking you through it, or you're going to hold it and wait for me. Which do you want to do?"

"I think I can go for it," I say with a confidence I'm certainly not feeling. "I just put a little bit on my cheeks like I did with the glitter on my eyes, right? How hard can that be?"

"If you think you can do it, go for it."

I open the compact and get a bit on my finger and go to dab it on my cheeks. "How'd I do?" I ask as I finish up with the glitter.

"Looks good princess, really good." They smile and I can see a faint blush appearing on their cheeks.

I look over the rest of the spread and my eyes land on a dark lipstick I've seen them wear before. "What if I even try a little bit of this?" I tease knowing that even if I do put some on, I'll immediately take it off.

"You think that's a good idea, princess? You want to try with something that dark?"

"I'll be able to see if I mess it up, and if I don't like it I can just take it off, right?"

"Well sometimes that one likes to stain, so the color might hang around for a few days. As long as that's not a problem for you."

"It can't be that bad." I take off the cap and roll up the tube. "It's got to be just like chapstick, right?"

"Kyle chapstick and lipstick are so completely different. You wouldn't want to start comparing the two."

I smile as I apply the lipstick the same way I would a chapstick, to their horror. When I look in the mirror my face is a complete mess. Do I really get chapstick everywhere when I apply it? Is it always that bad?

"What am I going to do with you?" They say as they gently bring the makeup wipe up to my lips and remove all of the lipstick, their eyes lingering on my lips. They're standing so close to me I can feel their breath on my cheeks and watch their cheeks flush a deeper shade of pink. They set the makeup wipe down and bring a hand up to run a finger over my bottom lip. Before I know it, they're kissing me.

They pull away from me, the blush on their cheeks brighter than ever.

"Oh my god! I'm so sorry! I don't know what came over me, I'm so sorry. I wasn't even thinking—"

I cut them off as I press my lips to theirs hoping they can see that I feel the same way about them as they do about me.

Before we know it it's time to get onstage and put on a damn good show.

Chapter Fourteen

The next morning I'm in the studio with Mari and Harper working on music. Harper and I are working through those two songs we had been writing and showing them to Mari for some feedback and tinkering with them. But I keep going back to the song I'm writing with Finn. I can't even focus on the conversation in front of me, the lyrics that they wrote constantly running through my mind:

Late nights all alone
Summer sun and telephones
In my darkest nights you held me close
I'd never want for you to go
Same dream, separate lives
Wonder if I'm always trailing behind
Then I see that look in your eyes

Harper and Mari are sat in a corner of the room going over the lyrics that Harper and I had written as I can't get Finn's lyrics out of my mind. When was I going to actually get to have a session with Finn? When were we going to get to have dedicated time to work on our song and not just whatever stolen moments we can seem to find?

On a fresh page of my notebook, I write down Finn's lyrics and start messing with them. I know I'm not good at this. I try a couple of different phrases trying to figure out what could come next. I don't know what Finn intends for part of the song to be, but maybe it's a good idea if it's the bridge. Or if it's the chorus that could work really well too.

I know I'm no songwriter, but maybe I can work something out with this so I can bring it to Finn tonight. If we get the chance to work on it tonight, I could bring this to them, and it could end up being really great. Maybe I can actually contribute something to the lyrics in a more concrete way, rather than just speaking and letting them piece together the words that I'm saying into a song.

I read over what Finn had written of the verse over and over and for some reason I just keep going back to the kiss last night. The kiss that I had so desperately wanted. It happened. And they wanted it too. But is kissing, and maybe even dating someone I work with even a good idea? We were friends first sure, *are* friends first, but now we're working together and seeing how awkward things have become with Stevie since the breakup with Finn, I know I don't want that to be a possibility for us, but maybe kissing Finn would be worth the awkwardness.

What if these lyrics are about me? Does the line *in my darkest nights you held me close* have anything to do with me? Could it be about those nights we spent writing that first song? Is there more that I didn't see that could be about me?

I scribble down a few different phrases and ideas to bring to Finn later. Maybe something there will actually be something they want to use. Maybe there will be something that becomes part of this song.

"Dude, are you even paying attention to anything we're saying?" Mari says as she shoves me, pulling me up from my notebook and bringing me back to the conversation at hand. "Harper's going to show me what the two of you have been working on."

"Oh. Sorry. I'm paying attention now," I say as I quickly shut the notebook before she can even take a look at the pages.

"What are you hiding in there?" Mari teases, reaching for the notebook as I pull it just out of her reach.

"It's nothing." I flip through the notebook to find what I had written for the songs I had been working on with Harper and grab my guitar from where it had been resting and started playing what we had been working on.

We started with the song that Harper had written and brought to me, and then we moved on to the song we had written together. Neither of the songs were exactly finished, but with Mari in the room with us, it was probably best to be looking for some more feedback on what we had been working on. Maybe she could even help us with the parts that we were struggling with.

It was weird though, playing a song that Harper and I wrote about our crushes and unrequited love after kissing Finn last night. The parts that I had written felt like they were so clearly about Finn it was insane. And playing those parts knowing they were going to hear it eventually was getting me excited to be able to share these songs with the rest of the band.

When we were done playing them for Mari, she had completely lit up and we immediately started working on those parts that we had been struggling with. Between stepping away from the songs for a bit and having another set of eyes looking at them, we were able to get so much further in the songs than we had initially. We would still need to bring them to the rest of the band and work it out in the group setting, but between the three of us, we had a pretty decent starting point for both of the songs and by the end of the session they should be ready to present to the rest of the band.

"So, I really, and I mean *really*, like that second song. The first one is good, and it's sweet and all, but that second one is filled with such raw emotion. It's really beautiful. I think the whole thing with like identity and not knowing who you are or who you're supposed to be is really going to resonate with our audience. It's really resonating with me," Mari says as she reads over the lyrics of the second song.

I smile, knowing Harper really took the reins on both of these songs, but also feeling a deep connection to that one in particular. "Yeah, I feel like this tour has been the first time I've really been away from home and have gotten a chance to, like, separate myself and who I want to be from the idea of who I am that my parents have. I don't know if it's the same for you, but I think that's something that really resonated with Harper and I." I smile at Harper. I know this room is a safe space for all of us, any room with the entire band generally is.

"Dude, your parents are insane. No wonder you feel

like you're figuring that shit out. You still don't even know how to dress," Mari says with a teasing smirk. "We need to take you shopping. I'm starting a Pinterest board for ideas."

I laugh as Mari takes out her phone. "Maybe we can do that later, and work on the songs instead. But that sounds like a good idea. It's all just so weird. Like I feel like I barely know who I am without my dad's constant control"

"He's had you under his thumb for so long. And he's not even letting you go far for college. Even moving out isn't really moving out. You're going to the school he wants, studying what he wants, and then once you graduate, you're going to be working the job he wants."

"He's not letting you be your own person," Harper chimes in for the first time.

"I know." I sigh. "The number of calls and texts I've been getting from him since we left is insane. I can't even post on my Instagram story without a text or phone call about what I'm wearing."

"Damn, that just made the song sadder," Mari frowns as she reads over the lyrics.

"Yeah. For me, I don't know, I feel like I'm just trying to figure out who I am outside of the band and my family. Not that I've had any kind of pressure like Kyle. I just…" Harper sighs. "I feel like the next four years are going to be a lot of that. A lot of learning who I am as a person."

"You? Really? You've always been so sure of yourself. You've known what you're doing, what school you wanted, what major you wanted, since we were little kids. Out of everyone here, you've always been the most sure of yourself." Mari shoots Harper a confused look.

"I've just been like figuring some things out that are changing my ten-year plan and it's a little scary."

I catch Harper's eye and send her a warm smile.

"What do you mean? You're like destined for the house in the suburbs with a husband and the white picket fence and two and a half kids. And a dog if you weren't allergic. What could possibly change that?"

Harper gets really quiet and looks down at her lap. She's playing with her rings and looks really nervous. "I'm gay." She says it softly, not even looking up. I immediately stand and cross the room so I'm sitting next to her. While this isn't news to me, I know that was still really hard for her and I want to be as supportive as possible.

"So, you're going to live in that two-story house in the suburbs with your wife and your two and a half kids," Mari says with a smile as she sits on the other side of Harper.

"I don't even know if I want that anymore. I don't know what I want anymore," Harper whispers as a tear slides down her cheek. I wrap an arm around her shoulder and give her a tight squeeze.

"You don't have to know that right now. You don't have to know anything right now," I say softly.

"I know. I just always thought I'd have that life where I live right outside of whatever city we end up in, and I'd find a husband and get married and do all the things that are expected of me. All the things that I've always thought I've wanted. But what if I don't? What if I get to college and I hate what I've been planning on majoring in and then it just throws everything I thought I knew into question?"

"Woah, hey, take a breath. You don't have to know any

of that right now. You don't even have to know what you're having for dinner. All you need to do is put one foot in front of the other and take everything one step at a time. You don't have to know what's going to happen ten years from now, or even ten months, ten days, ten hours, or ten minutes. None of us do," I say trying to be comforting.

"But I always do! And now all of a sudden everything is changing! What the hell am I supposed to do?" Harper's now fully spiraling, and I don't know what else I can say to help.

"Hey. Look at me," Mari says, taking over. "Kyle's right. You don't have to know shit about your future. But what you do need to know is being gay changes nothing. Gay or not you are still the same person you were ten minutes ago because, news flash, you've been gay this whole time. And we all know change is scary, but you need to allow for this change to happen for you to be happy. You're not going to be happy forcing yourself into this role that is just not fit for you."

"And do you know what will help?" I chime in, trying to bring the conversation back to focus. "The song still doesn't have a bridge." I pick up her pen and hand it to her before getting up to pick up my guitar. "Channel all that fear and write the bridge."

Harper nods and we get to work writing the bridge and, before we know it, Stevie is pulling us into a bigger room with Finn and Aspen so we can start working through what we've written.

We all sit on the floor of the room and start to trade songs around, everyone taking turns sharing what they've been working on and collaborating on songs where necessary. While there are a few songs that we decided we're going to use but need to keep working on, we all decide as a group that the song Harper and I wrote, the one about changing and coming to terms with who we are, is going to be the first song we record.

We get to meet briefly with the recording technicians who work at the studio before we all start to get set up for a little bit of writing and working on some of the other songs while we take turns recording our sections. Deciding that we were going to record the song Harper and I had written really puts the whole process into gear.

Maybe the hardest thing about traveling and touring while working on this album is the change in people at every stop. One day this is going to be able to feel like a real job. A job where we go into the same "office" every day, seeing the same people, and doing relatively the same thing. One day, we'll be able to just walk into the same studio on the days we're working and know everyone else who works there. We won't be meeting new people and entering into new spaces every single time we go in to work on an album. One day. Hopefully.

We get ourselves situated and comfortable in a pretty big room as most of us began to tune our instruments and warm up and do whatever else we needed to do to be prepared for the few hours of playing before our show tonight.

We decided to finish up writing a different song while Harper went into the other room to start recording for the song. We had just a bit more to go before we could start hopping into the booth and record this one, so we just dive right in playing through what we already had written just to hear how it sounds and figure out where we wanted to go with it next, as we were gearing up to write the bridge.

We start playing from the beginning, I hear a few little things that need changing, smoothing out, that we could work on even before touching the bridge. As we hit the first chorus, I'm not sure I really like the sound of it, and in the middle of the first chorus I decide to just switch up what I'm playing until I find something I'm happier with. Mari keeps shooting me weird looks as I fiddle with what I'm playing until we get to the second verse. By that point the song is flowing so much smoother, and I think we are all pretty happy with the trajectory of the song as we head into the second chorus.

By the time we are finished with what we had already written, I'm itching to keep going. I don't even fully stop when everyone else does, playing on as I found my rhythm of what I think could be cool for the bridge.

When I finally stop playing and look up, everyone is staring at me.

"Did I do something?" I ask looking up at the rest of my bandmates.

"Yes. But not like that, maybe just play that again," Aspen says softly, looking at me expectantly. I nod and begin to play it again. "I like that. How does everyone else feel? Do we want to run with that?"

Looking around the group there are a chorus of nods and hums of approval. I'm doing something right.

"Okay, wait. First, Kyle write that down. Whatever you just did, however you need to remember what you just did. Do it. Then before we really dive into the bridge, Kyle was doing something funky during the chorus. I think we need to explore that first," Mari says, barely taking her eyes off of me. I nod and flip to a new page in my notebook.

"Funky good or funky bad?" I ask Mari, genuinely unsure of how it is being received and what she means. "Good. I think. But I think I need to hear it again just to be sure." Mari smiles at me, as I began to play what I had played during the first run through of the song.

"Wait, I really like that," Finn said when I finish, smiling as they look toward the rest of our bandmates for their input.

"I really like it, but is there a way we could make it… more?" Aspen says, looking to Mari for help or approval, I can't really tell.

"More what?" I ask, trying to understand what she's saying. More could mean so many different things, and I think I get what she's trying to get at, but I'm just not one hundred percent sure.

"I don't know. Bigger, I guess. It feels like it's just almost there but not quite. Like, I do really like it, but I feel like there's something we can do to make it feel bigger if that makes sense."

I nod, fully understanding now, and I think I might have an idea that could work.

"Okay, yeah." Mari picks up her bass. "Kyle, play it again. I want to try something."

I play the chorus again as Mari begins to add her own spin on what I was doing with her own instrument. Then Aspen makes her way over to the keyboard to replicate what we were doing. And it's working, I think. I try to also amp it up a bit. Letting myself be looser with what I'm playing. Make it feel more intense. And I think I'm doing it.

We get to the end of the chorus, and I look to Aspen and Mari to see if we have accomplished what Aspen had in mind and her smile says everything I need to hear. We're getting somewhere with this.

"I think that's it, but can I hear it with drums too? I just want to get a full feel for it."

Finn nods and heads back to the drum set and we play the chorus for a third time.

"Yes! That's it!" Aspen cheers as we finish. I can't help the proud smile that spreads across my cheeks. It's nice getting to actually write as a group. We haven't had a whole lot of time where we've been really working on the album as a group and even though Harper isn't here, it feels really good to be working on this as a band. After all, the album is something created by all of us.

"Okay, yeah. I think I've got that." Mari smiles as she writes something in her notebook. "Should we get back to the bridge now? Or is there more that's needed before we can get over there?"

I look between the rest of my bandmates, the issues I've been having with our first verse seems to have ironed itself out by the second, now that we've got the chorus to a really good place and I'm ready to start working on the bridge if everyone else is.

"Yeah. I think we're good to move on to the bridge," Finn says, taking control of the situation and steering us in the direction we need.

The four of us relax and we began writing the bridge.

Chapter Fifteen

Going back to our hotel room that night felt like such a treat. I'm beyond exhausted. Songwriting and recording, while fun, uses so much energy. Especially when working on songs that feel so personal. It is just so draining writing about my biggest insecurities like that.

At some point while in the studio, I had posted a few Instagram stories of us working. Nothing that would be giving anything away, but just enough to be a fun teaser for the fans. Something to let them know that we're working on something new for them.

The response from the fans was perfect, honestly. The excitement is growing, and it just feels really cool to be an artist who can show little bits and tease like that while also pulling the "we can't talk about it" card.

But of course, every single post comes with a message from my father, even when it's just a story. Because I still haven't taken the nail polish off. Honestly, I didn't even realize my hand was in the photo. But even if it wasn't he probably would have found something else to comment on. Something else to be upset about.

Dad

DAD

I thought we talked about the nail polish.

KYLE

What does it matter?

It's just a little bit of paint

no one else cares

DAD

People do care

You're practically asking to be harassed

KYLE

you're being overdramatic

DAD

just take it off

KYLE

if I can remember to I will. We've been pretty busy

DAD

that's no excuse

KYLE

okay.

I throw down my phone after sending that last text hoping it satisfies him as Finn heads into the bathroom and that's when I see it sitting on the dresser. Another letter. Of course. I snatch it before Finn comes out of the bathroom and this time, I don't even open it before crumpling it up and throwing it in my backpack. I don't care to read it this time. It doesn't even mean anything, not when Finn and I are some form of together.

Later Finn and I start to work on that other song that they had started working on. I show them some of the tweaks I made, and we talk for hours, working bits of conversation into the lyrics as they love to do, and the song starts to take shape. The last song we wrote together was fun, but this one feels special. There's something in this song that has me unable to put it down or put it out of my head. We work on it all night.

♫

After a full day of writing and reworking the song, Finn and I were ready to bring it to the girls. Our song. Our baby.

As was to be expected, I was incredibly nervous. We had just a few hours booked to work on some writing for the album before some of us were heading in to record and there's a good chance we could be going in to record this song that Finn and I have poured our hearts, souls, and relationship into.

I want to hold Finn's hand as we bring the song to the rest of our band, for nothing more than simple comfort. But I know I shouldn't do that. We haven't even put a label on whatever this is that we're doing together, not that I would mind a label of any sort, I just don't want to push Finn into something they aren't ready for.

We know that the best way for us to bring the song to the girls would be for us to perform it for them, even though going into it we both know that the song isn't going to be perfect. Good enough is enough for us.

We sit in the room with the girls and I pull out my acoustic guitar as Finn sits at the makeshift drum set that we had set up in the small space. My hands are shaking as I make sure my guitar is in tune and I try my best to just put it out of my mind. We're just playing a song. It's totally not a song that has all of the feelings Finn and I have been feeling towards each other over these last few weeks. Nothing like that at all.

"Kyle and I have actually been working on another song together over the past few weeks. It's not much and it's far from perfect, but could we maybe just show y'all what we've got and maybe work on it from there?"

I hate how nervous and unsure of themself they sound. I look over at them and smile in a way I could only hope was reassuring.

Mari nearly flies out of her seat in excitement at the idea that we had been working on something together, claiming we're her favorite ship out of the whole band. I just have to laugh at that. We've barely done interviews, or any press for that matter, what could we possibly be putting out into the world that could give fans that idea? Were we acting too close on stage and on social media? Was it that obvious? Or was it just the fans coming up with something that has no ground? Maybe I need to spend more time on social media looking into it.

Once Harper gets Mari to settle down, Finn and I get

the chance to play our song. Sitting on the floor while playing has become oddly comforting for me and so I sit on the floor as Finn counts me in. My fingers find their places on the frets of my instrument as I pluck each string in perfect succession. The two of us together play music in a way we have never done before. It feels so real, raw and intense. It makes me feel so in love with my drummer. I can't help but want this moment to last forever.

Sure, throughout the song we stumble a bit. That was going to happen regardless though. It's to be expected. We've barely even gotten to a point where we're comfortable playing something we've only just written in front of others. Neither of us are the most confident of writers, but we tried our best.

We start at the beginning with the first verse, and as we play and sing through the whole thing, I keep my eyes locked on Finn's only glancing down once at my notebook as I stumble over a few words and try my best to laugh it off as we launch into the first chorus.

By the time we get to the end of the first chorus the confidence I normally feel when playing is back with full force. It's like someone flipped a switch and I'm me again in the wildest of ways. I'm playing the song with the full force and intensity the song needs and deserves, and it feels so good. It feels so right to be playing the song that Finn and I wrote for each other and when I close my eyes I can just picture us playing on stage in front of crowds even bigger than we're playing for now.

When we finish playing, I hesitantly look up at the girls hoping for some kind of positive reaction, but there was no way for me to have expected anything close to what we get. Mari, Harper, and Aspen all look teary eyed and choked up. For a moment, there is a part of me that just thinks they really hated the song, but then I lock eyes with Harper and when she speaks, I know we have something special.

She looks at Finn and I with tears shining in her eyes and whispers: "I think I know what song I want to be our first single."

I look to Finn in disbelief. Is that even a possibility? This song, this one song that has been our little back burner project. The song that we've been pouring over in the hopes that maybe something the two of us have worked together on would actually make it onto the album after the not-so-great reaction to the last song we brought to the band. *This* is the song that could be our first single.

Finn gets up from the drum set and sits down next to me, grabbing my hand and squeezing it gently. Our song is going to be something special. We've written something really special.

"Of course, there's some work to do on the song still," Mari cuts in. "But that's partly on expanding it to be some-thing that we can play all five of us and not just the two of you. We can take the rest of this studio time to work on it, if you'd like. We probably won't have to do too much with the song itself, maybe just some light tinkering. I maybe have a few areas where I could improve on the lyrics, but what you have is really great and I want to capitalize off of that as best as we can. What the two of you wrote together is really special, please don't lose that in all the tinkering we're about to do."

Mari beams at us, and I truly feel as if we did some-thing right.

"But I do have to ask, seeing how y'all are looking at each other and the lyrics of the song you clearly wrote together. What is going on between the two of you?" Aspen asks bluntly and I can't help but pause. "Are y'all like together?"

"We, um…" I start to say, looking to Finn to see how they want to handle this. "I think we…"

"Yeah. We are," Finn says as I stumble over my words trying to figure out how to say that without saying it. "But can we keep it quiet? It's still really new. And I'd rather we didn't tell Stevie right now." When they add that, I feel a sense of relief wash over me. It's exactly what I needed to hear to feel confident with what has just started between us.

Everyone looks a little shocked at Finn's request at first. It's not one any of us were expecting, I wasn't even expecting it. But at the same time, Finn and I haven't even had a conversation about what our relationship is. Not to mention they just got out of a relationship with Stevie not too long ago. I don't blame them for wanting to take things slow and keeping it quiet for now, even though I want more than anything to just scream it from the rooftops and tell everyone that we're together. I want to be excited about this and have fun with it, but I understand where they're coming from with that, and I have to respect it.

"Are you sure we should be keeping this from Stevie?" Harper asks tentatively.

"I'd really rather she didn't know. At least not yet. With the way everything went down, I'm not sure telling her I'm in a new relationship is going to be the best course of action. She's been staring at me enough as is," Finn says as they pull their hand out of mine. I frown slightly at the emptiness it leaves, but it's not up for discussion. At least not here in this semi-public setting.

So, we move on to work on the song that Finn and I wrote together. Though, knowing it can be difficult for us to all work together on the song as a group of five, with multiple different instruments, Mari sends Harper and Aspen off to work together on the keys and vocals, and maybe tinker with the words a bit, while she works with Finn and I on her part. While her and Finn make up the sort of rhythm to any song we play, her and I also need to be in sync with one another. And these groupings always work well when it comes to fine tuning any song that we've written for the band. At this point we're like a well-oiled machine. We've spent years working together both in and out of school and we've gotten to a pretty good place with how we're working together.

We spend about two hours together just crafting the bass part. It was almost as if each world, each syllable even, is something we need to go over. Something we have to shape. But in the end, it's perfect. The song is perfect. We are perfect.

Once we feel the song is ready to be recorded, we loop Stevie in and bring her in on our idea. Stevie immediately has us start getting ready to record and ushers Harper into the booth while keeping the rest of us in the little room to keep on writing and working on the album.

I move back to the floor, seemingly my favorite place to write, and start messing around with a chord progression we have been working with for one of the songs Aspen and Harper had written together. The two of them kept their focus on their lyrics and the melody and somehow working the melody into the instrumentation fell to me. At least it's the one part of song writing that I love and that I think I'm pretty good at, if I do say so myself. I had barely gotten a chance to look at what had been written as I was starting so it wasn't much, not yet at least, but the four of us seem to be completely in sync with one another as we work. Mari and Aspen try some lyrics for the bridge which hasn't been written yet, though we really all seem to feel Harper's absence.

"It's weird trying to write without Harper," Aspen says with a frown after twenty minutes. "She always knows exactly what the lyrics need. I can't even tell what story we're trying to tell, if one at all." I can see she's getting frustrated. It can't be easy working on lyrics for a song that she's been writing with Harper without Harper actually being present, even if the songs are all a group effort among the five of us. It's hard to really keep it so that every one of us is working on the songs. Sometimes it just feels like there's too many cooks in the kitchen.

"We're always trying to tell some kind of story, we'll figure it out," Mari says. "Let's just look at it again. You have creative control here. You've started on the words. What are you trying to say?" I can tell Mari is just trying to be helpful, but I look at Aspen and can see her eyes starting to get watery. "Aspen, you don't need to give us the full story, but a little context could be helpful," Mari says, this time softer and gentler as if she can sense the panic starting to seep into Aspen's mind.

"Loving someone who doesn't love you back," Aspen whispers after a few minutes.

"Good. We can work with that. You don't need to say who, I think I know, but you don't need to say." I didn't think it was possible for Aspen to turn an even darker shade of red, but she somehow manages to. "What kind of vibe do you want for the song? How do you want it to sound?"

We go on for a while like that, Mari asking Aspen prompting questions to get her to say what she wants for the song so it can be written the way she wants it to be. Eventually it gets to the point where we're getting somewhere, but then Harper comes back into the room and it's my turn to go record for the song Finn and I had written, Summer Sunsets.

I head back into the main recording room, leaving my acoustic guitar with my bandmates in favor of my electric.

The technicians help me get all set up and comfortable. I start standing up, as that was the most normal way to be recording and I guess also the most natural. Even though I had been sitting on the floor for our writing sessions, I feel for the recording that I want to be able to move more freely. Well, as freely as I could with about a hundred wires attached to me. I just want to be able to move with the music in a more compacted sense to what's it's going to be like onstage.

Once everything is hooked up, the technician goes back into his booth with all of the electronic recording equipment and computers, and we begin to do a sound check. On top of recording guitar, I'm also adding a few harmonies to the song. It's such a small part of each and every song, but depending on the song it could be me, Mari, or Aspen. Sometimes it's a combination of the three of us, or just two of us, depending on whatever the song needs.

Regardless, I always find this part to be really fun, even if it is insanely tedious. Sometimes I have to do the same small thing a hundred different times in a hundred different ways before we get it right, but when I do it right for the first time that feeling is unmatched. And then, getting to hear all of it come together as I help mix and produce the songs is one of my favorite parts of this whole process, for sure.

We start with recording my guitar parts. We want it to sound really full, but not too full to the point where we wouldn't be able to get close to recreating the sound on a stage eventually.

I played through the same part of the song a few times before we had something we really liked the sound of. Then we got to messing around with different levels of distortion until we had it to the levels that we felt were best for the song. I make a note of it, to remember for when we get to play the song live. After we were happy with that, we then move on to recording the little fun bits and guitar riffs I'll get to include in the song. For me, this was probably the most fun part of the recording process. Not every song would have something like this included in it, but having a little bit included can make the show more fun for me.

I play through the sections of the song that we think might be a good spot for a little guitar riff or something that sounds cool and I just keep playing those chords over and over as I try different things until something sticks. It's fun but it is also so hard. At one point, one of the technicians comes in and starts playing with me, as he goes through a few different ideas and helps me come to one that is subtle enough for the song but going to be really fun to play live. The perfect combination.

When I'm done, I'm asked to send Finn in. I walk back

into the room where the rest of the band has been sitting and working and walk up behind Finn and wrap my arms around their neck. I lean in and whisper in their ear and I don't miss the shiver that runs down their spine.

I look up after planting a soft kiss on their cheek to see Mari with her phone out, clearly having just taken a picture of us. I raise an eyebrow at her, and she passes me her phone.

"I was thinking of posting one, not the one of you kissing Finn, obviously, that one I took just for y'all to have, but only if you're cool with it," she says with an innocent smile, though nothing about what she's just said is innocent. I turn the phone to Finn, and we look through the pictures Mari had taken when we were unaware and completely wrapped up in each other and they are truly amazing.

There is one picture that looks like it could just be us working, and if any of them are going to be posted my vote goes to that one. I know my dad will see it, and that picture will give me the least amount of backlash from him. And I do still have to be thinking about that, unfortunately.

Finn scrolls through the pictures again and then picks one, luckily, it's the one I would've picked too, handing the phone back to Mari. "That's my favorite social media appropriate one." They smile and I pull them in for a real kiss before sending them out to go record.

"The two of you are really cute together, actually. I get what everyone on the internet is saying," Aspen said after a beat of silence.

"Oh, are we now?" I reply with a smirk, pulling out my phone to look through the fan accounts on social media to see that of course there are fans shipping us. There are a handful shipping Harper and Aspen too. They pull all sorts of clips from different interviews and videos that we've all posted that fit the narrative they're trying to push. I can't help but love it.

"I mean, look at the two of you. Who wouldn't want that?" Aspen looks to Harper for the briefest of seconds and blushes ever so slightly. I lock eyes with Mari and mouth a quick "Am I missing something?" and she just smiles back at me. I scroll to a video edit of the two of them and maybe it's just the fan's creativity, but I can't help but see something that may or may not be there.

"It's nice to not have to be so secretive about it anymore. I just… I really like them. And I'm so happy." I smile dreamily.

"Someone's clearly whipped," Mari says with a smile. "But I do have to say it, Kyle, if you hurt them, I will end you. I hope you know that."

I laugh, knowing Finn and Mari have been close since well before I even moved into our hometown.

"You're not coming to my defense?" I ask, feigning offense,, but in the end her loyalties should lie with Finn who she's known much longer.

"Oh, come on, Kyle. We both know you don't need me. You've got your girls." She smirks, referring to my best friend and cousin back home.

"Yeah, that's true. I'm honestly scared for the next time Finn sees Perri and Aubrey. Perri might kill them on the spot." I joke, but knowing how protective Perri can be, is it really a joke or just a fact?

"It's a shame it took so long for her to move near to us, I think I'd have been really good friends with her if we had more time. But she's always so attached to Aubrey's hip. Not that there's anything wrong with Aubrey, I love the girl, you know I do, but I never got the chance to really have some alone time with Perri."

"The two of you are very similar. Though I'm not sure that's a good thing."

"It's whatever you want it to be."

I roll my eyes as Mari continues to tease me.

"I'm loving this, I really am, but we've only got another thirty minutes here before we need to head to the venue. So can we wrap up whatever this is and get back to our work?" Harper says pulling Mari and I from whatever little world we're in.

"Right. Yeah. Sorry. What did I miss?" I say as I find my way back to my spot on the floor.

Aspen, Harper, and Mari spend the next fifteen minutes or so filling me in on what I had missed, teaching me the very basic guitar part that was written for me. By the time I was finished learning my part, Finn was coming back into the room, and we started packing up to head to the venue.

Chapter Sixteen

We arrive at the venue way earlier than we expected. We've generally had some form of down time throughout our days, but these past few have just been so jam-packed that we really haven't had a moment to breathe. This newfound free time has us all unsure of what to do. Mari suggests we come together in one of the dressing rooms and go live on Instagram for a little bit to interact with our fans before the show.

We all sit together, getting comfortable on the couch. I almost pull Finn onto my lap but realize that would probably be taking things just a step too far and settle for having them next to me on the couch. Mari's on my other side, while Aspen and Harper sit on either end of the couch on the armrests.

Mari gets the phone all set up so that we can still read it, but it has all of us in frame and once we are all ready, she starts the livestream, and we wait for fans and friends to join.

"Hi everyone!" Mari says as people start to join, and the comments start rolling in. I just sit there awkwardly for a few minutes not sure of what I'm supposed to be doing.

"How is everyone?" Finn asks and the comments go wild.

"We just had some extra time before our show tonight here in Salt Lake City, so we thought we'd go live and maybe answer some questions," Harper says with a big smile on her face.

"Someone just said 'we're outside let us in', we can't yet. Doors don't open for two more hours," Mari says with a laugh and a smile towards the camera. "If we had control over that we would. But stay hydrated, it's hot out there."

"Are people really lining up already?" Aspen asks, sounding almost nervous.

"Well apparently, I guess," I say, looking to Stevie just out of frame who just nods confirming that there is already a line forming outside of the venue.

"Do they just really want to get a good spot or what? I mean I know it's all general admission, but we do have some people with the meet and greet before the show," Mari says looking towards Finn and I.

"I guess. I mean I knew people did that for like bigger artists when they have GA tickets and want to get close to the stage. I guess I never thought people would be doing that for us." I laugh and gently put a hand on Finn's knee. How is it even possible that we have fans that want to line up for hours outside of the venue to just try and get on the barricade. That's insane dedication.

"Yeah, I guess," Mari says with a sigh. "Kyle, you have got to be careful where you're putting your hand. People are going feral in the chat."

"I just put my hand on Finn's knee. Is that not a normal thing to do?" I blush as I pull my hand away.

"I think we need to educate you on what normal friends do." Mari teases and if it is possible for my cheeks to go even redder, they do. Finn's do too.

"Oh really. Do we now?" I try to keep that light, teasing lilt to my voice, but I see Stevie out of the corner of my eye, and she looks pissed. My guess is that she's not too happy with the closeness between Finn and I, she never liked it when they were together, but somehow now it's worse.

"We need to educate you on a lot of things, princess," Finn says with a laugh as the comments start to go wild at the nickname. If we want to keep this private maybe we should stop feeding into it, but it's just too much fun.

"Don't go doing that. You're going to start something we really don't need." I shoot them a teasing glare as I think about the fanfiction that is going to be written from this very moment.

"Am I now?"

I roll my eyes but can't help the smile that spreads across my face. "Finn, you've been calling me princess for years. It's just an inside joke. We can't go giving people ideas, now, can we?"

"We've always been weirdly close, that's all the ideas we're giving them." Finn smiles at me feigning innocence.

"Yeah, sure. Whatever you need to tell yourself to get you to sleep at night." I smile sweetly back at them. "Anyways, we should answer some questions before we have to hop off and get ready."

"Right. We do have to make sure your makeup is perfect, princess." I blush again as I see a few feral comments from my cousin as she reacts to the makeup comment. I will be fielding texts about that later for sure.

I laugh and shove Finn who just cackles, leaving Harper to reel us in and ask some of the questions coming through the chat that she did feel we could actually answer.

The conversation then turned to talking about our music and what was potentially coming for the band. All of our little studio story posts have been gaining as much traction as a story post can, I think, at least they have with our fans, and they are very ready to listen to some new music from us. I can't wait to finish this album and get it out. We only have a week left on tour, a week that we're going to spend every single second of free time dedicated to the album, but we might not be making the deadline.

There are some funny questions too about all sorts of random things about our lives. It's fun getting to know our fanbase in this way, and it is really fun until a comment caught my eye.

"@perrs0605 is asking, when she can expect a call back, Kyle?" Finn says, reading the comment out loud with a smile.

"Oh, she wants to know when she can expect a call back does she?" I laugh. "Well, hi Perri. I'll call you back when I feel like it. Clearly, I'm busy."

Finn and Mari both laughed at that while Harper and Aspen looked at me confused.

"That's my cousin." I smile as I clarify. They just nod and move on to the next question. "I'll call you soon."

We sit on Instagram live for about an hour before we have to head back to the dressing rooms to start getting ready for the show. The live was long and relatively taxing in a way I hadn't expected it to be. There's something about being live on social media and having to be on and giving one hundred percent for the fans and followers while focusing on the chat, and not talking over each other, letting everyone get a chance to speak, and listening to what each other is saying. It all just takes a lot of brain power, and more energy than I had anticipated.

When I walk into the dressing room with Finn, what I really want to do is take a nap, but I know I don't have the time. Though I quickly forget about my exhaustion when Finn closes the door and pulls me onto our couch.

"Hi," they breathe as they pull themself onto my lap before kissing me deeply and passionately. "I've missed you so much."

"Baby, you've been with me all day," I mumble.

"But I haven't been able to do this." They plant a soft kiss on my lips. "Or this," one on my throat, "and especially not this." They grin devilishly at me as they kiss me on the sensitive spot right behind my left ear that sends a shiver down my spine.

"Yeah? I'm sure the girls wouldn't have minded," I joke, but we both know doing that in front of Stevie is beyond off limits.

"Oh, you think you're funny now, don't you princess?" Finn smirks, pulling away ever so slightly so that I'm forced to look them dead in the eye.

"Hilarious, actually." I smirk back as I snake my arms around their waist.

"Are you now? I hadn't noticed." I swat at their shoulder lightly as they tease me.

"You hadn't? That's such a shame. It's only part of my charm."

They scoff in surprise as we continue to tease each other. "Is it now?"

"I like to think it is. Are you saying it's not?"

"No, I'm just saying there are other things about you that I find to be very charming." They actually think I'm charming?

"Oh, so you think I'm charming?" I say taking the win.

"Of course I do, princess." I smile and give them a quick kiss before they're pulling away.

"Where are you going?" I pout.

"Princess, we've got a show to do."

"But," I make grabby hands begging for them to come back.

"No buts, we can do more of this after the show, princess." Finn smiles at me before changing into their show outfit. I went over to my bag in the corner and pulled out my own outfit.

After getting dressed, I pulled out all of the makeup and got started on my eyeshadow. While I was standing in front of the mirror putting on my glitter, I felt Finn come up behind me and wrap their arms around my waist.

"Hi baby," I whisper as I continue to apply the makeup.

"You look so pretty tonight, princess." They smile, pressing a kiss to my shoulder.

"So do you," I put the brush down and relax into them. "We should go out tonight then. Show me off all pretty like this."

"Oh, you're such a flirt."

"Sure, but we could still use a date night. Pizza and diner food is getting boring."

"Are you asking me on a date?"

"Would that be a problem?"

"Not at all. You can pick me up from the hotel right after the show." They pause and sigh, shooting me an apologetic smile. "If we can get Stevie to sign off on it."

"Who said we need her to sign off on it?"

♬

We start the next morning doing yet another photoshoot. Though this one is supposed to be for our album cover. A shoot for an album that we have barely pieced together. It feels almost too soon, but it's not something we get to really have control over, so we just go along with it as Stevie ushers us into the van.

There are concepts for the shoot and for the album cover that really just come down to color. At this point in the process for us, we don't know what we actually want this album to be, conceptually. I guess, to some degree we have an idea as to what type of music we want to put out and the kind of music we're writing, but other than that we haven't yet decided what we want to say with the album. For us, in this moment, the album is such a work in progress that it's maybe half written. How are the five of us supposed to make serious creative decisions like this when we barely even know what we're creating?

The one thing we could all agree on, especially now that we've decided that the song Finn and I wrote, Summer Sunsets, is going to be the first single off of the album, and maybe even the title track, is that the color palette is going to be that of a sunset.

With the lack of conceptual ideas for the album itself, this is at least one thing that feels really concrete. We have decided that we're going to do the shoot on a black background with the five of us dressed head to toe each in a different color of a sunset color palette.

Aspen will be posed on the far left in an orangey yellow outfit, with Finn next to her in orange, Harper in the middle in a pinky orange shade, then me in a deeper pink, and Mari on the very end in purple. And each of us is wearing a makeup look that matches the colors of our outfits. With a lot of glitter.

We have a couple of different ideas as for poses. There are a few where we are all just kind of standing in the space almost awkwardly, and then a few that have us just standing together and interacting with each other in a type of way. Each different pose is shot in what feels like a dozen different ways.

There's another concept that we decide to try as well. It's more of a party type scene, with lots of glitter and balloons. And then a few with confetti.

By the end of the shoot, we're all covered in glitter, and I can't speak for anyone else, but I'm incredibly sweaty. Though the shoot is fun, maybe even more fun than the one we did for that magazine earlier in the month. Maybe that's just because the shoot is for the band as a whole so there's a whole lot less waiting around for our turn and a whole lot more time spent in the action of the shoot.

We then get to spend some time looking over different fonts to decide what we might want to use, before leaving it up to the photographers and editors and all the people to decide what is going to look best and what we should want on our album cover. There will be a handful of different options presented to us so we can have the final decision, and then if we decide to do a deluxe version with more songs or different variants for different stores with different album covers, we will have plenty of options.

Chapter Seventeen

After what feels like forever and days of endless working, we are lucky enough to have our first real day off. Finn and I actually got to sleep in. We weren't being carted off to shows and interviews and photoshoots and all sorts of meetings. Today was just going to be a great day to act like a tourist in this new city and just have fun together. It just so happens that we are in this beautiful city and performing during their wonderful pride weekend. Of course, Finn and I are going to go out to celebrate. And now that we've kissed, and both admitted to having feelings for each other, we can just go and have fun and just be together.

Finn nearly jumps out of bed full of excitement for the day ahead the second my alarm goes off at nine thirty. I know nine thirty isn't much of a sleep-in, but after spending the past few weeks having to get up between five and six thirty, it's a welcome reprieve. I stay in bed for a little while longer, drinking in the warmth and comfort from the queen-sized hotel bed while I watch Finn run back and forth between their suitcase and the bathroom as they keep changing their outfit until they settle on a really cute mesh top and some jeans. As they start on their makeup, I finally pull myself out of bed and put on my normal ripped jeans and the only cropped band tee I own.

I hesitate putting the top on, knowing we're going out in public. I've tried wearing this top out once before and I did really like how it looked on me. I felt really confident and cool in it. I had been hyping myself up for what felt like weeks to feel confident enough to wear this top. But I never left my room. I shouldn't have bought it, really. It was a stupid purchase, honestly. I don't know what I was thinking. I know my dad. I know what he would say if he saw me in it. I know wearing it will never go well. But it's pride, and I want to just feel as cool and confident as I had when I first tried it on. I can't be a teen if I'm not rebelling in one way or another, right?

When the top ended up in my suitcase, I honestly wasn't sure it was a good idea. I don't even know how I ended up packing it. I guess a small part of me thought I wouldn't be at my dad's mercy so much now that I'm not living with him, but I know going home is only going to be hell and wearing this top out in public is only going to make that worse. But maybe a few rough weeks at home is worth the confidence I'm feeling right now. Maybe it'll be worth all the comments and snide remarks. Maybe my dad will even be proud of me. No, that will never happen, but maybe he'll learn to be okay with this?

I then go to put on some makeup. Or, more accurately, cover myself in glitter and eyeliner doing my very best without consulting Finn for help. They taught me how to do it, and even though I know I'm not the best at it, I just want to make them proud.

Finn comes out of the bathroom to see me lacing up my docs and their jaw nearly hits the floor. "Wow," they say breathlessly as their eyes roam over my body.

"Is that a good wow?" I ask tentatively, picking at my nail polish. Part of me worrying their reaction was going to be just like my dad's, even though I know deep down they would never.

They cross the room making their way over to me. "Yeah, it's a good wow. That top looks fabulous on you, princess," they say in a low whisper as they wrap their arms around my waist and give me a quick peck before they turn to pack up the small bag they're bringing for the day.

We get to the parade early with the goal to be as close to the front as possible if we're lucky—and we are, we get to be standing right up against the barricade. I don't think I could have asked for a better pride experience. Standing at the front, we get to see everything.

The sidewalk feels so empty when we arrive. There's barely anyone actually here for the parade. For the first fifteen or twenty minutes we see people just passing by, I guess that's to be expected when we showed up an hour early.

To be fair, it was Finn's fault that we showed up a whole hour early. They wanted to wake up extremely early to start getting ready. Maybe I should have. It could have been nice getting to spend more time with them alone in our hotel room, but there was a part of me that was eager to get here and show off my newfound confidence. Really, I wanted to go a pride event with my partner and get to really just celebrate as a queer person. But not being able to hold their hand was pure torture. By the time the event started, there was nothing I wanted more than to just hold my boyfriend's hand in this crowd of queer people. I wanted to be one of them. But I couldn't help but feel like there were tons of eyes on us at all times. People were watching us. People knew us. Should we have even come?

Not too long before the parade starts, we find ourselves next to a very wonderful and kind older lesbian couple. They introduced themselves as Tara and Amelia. And, to be fair, when I say older, I do just mean older than us. They were in their late twenties or early thirties. By typical social standards they were young, but to us, two eighteen-year-olds out in the world for the very first time, it felt as though they were older people taking us under their wings. After finding out it was our first pride, they were eager to make sure we had the best time imaginable.

The parade itself feels magical. For starters, I've never been around so many gay people in my life. And the whole thing is just filled with an immense sense of love and joy, and I want to stay there forever. Every single time I look over to Finn they have the biggest smile on their face, like they too wish they could stay there forever.

We happened to have gotten a really great spot where we get to see most of the action and all the fabulous performers. There are so many beautiful drag queens and kings. There are people giving free mom hugs and just being the kindest of human beings. It's all so much to take in. Everywhere I look there's something else happening or something to look at or just people wearing really cool outfits.

By the time we're leaving with Tara and Amelia to

head to a party they had invited us to, I've got a pride flag tied around my neck like a cape and am nearly covered in rainbow glitter. I've posted a dozen stories on Instagram and filled my social media with pride content, which might have been a mistake as there were a handful of fans that used my stories to come find us and take pictures, but it didn't bother me in the slightest. It's really just so nice and so cool to be part of something like this and to say that we were here. We were at this pride. We got to see those performers. Maybe one day we'll get to perform at a pride event. How cool would that be?

As we move through the crowd after the parade Finn grabs my hand. Logically, I know it was just so that they won't lose me in the crowd, but there is a small part of me that just wants to let myself believe that it is just simply holding hands with my partner in public.

We follow Tara and Amelia to the house party they invited us to, and I check my phone, unsurprised to see a slew of angry texts from my dad.

Dad

DAD

I saw your stories

What the hell do you think you're doing

Kyle I'm serious

I thought we had a conversation about you not doing this in public

I better not see pictures of this tomorrow

I thought I raised you better than this

I shove my phone back into my pocket and decide the best course of action is going to be to ignore the texts, and when I feel my phone vibrate with a call, I don't answer it. I'm here to have a good time, not spend my first ever pride event getting yelled at by my dad.

Finn and I move through the space together with a confidence neither of us was used to having. We each grab a drink as we move through the house trying to figure out what exactly we're doing. We are in a new space where no one knows us, where we can be whoever we want. In my inebriated state, I can't seem to keep my hands off Finn, especially now that this line between us has been crossed.

We find a dark corner where we are able to enjoy the music in our own way, dancing with each other while not feeling overwhelmed and stifled by the crowd. Their hands find my bare waist and they simply hold me there in a way that made me feral. Their touch alone has to be lethal.

"I don't know how much longer I'll be able to keep from kissing you when you keep touching me like that," I whisper in Finn's ear, hoping it comes across teasingly. This whole thing is new for us, and we've only just started kissing or whatever this is, but even so, it feels like it had been a long time coming.

"Like this?" They ask with a smirk as the tips of their fingers lightly graze my bare stomach and I can't help but shiver slightly at their touch.

"Just like that," I practically purr in their ear.

"It's not like you're making it easy for me, princess," they said with that smirk still spread across their lips. "Not with you wearing that." They look up at me and bite their lip and it is over for me.

I can confidently say that I am not in control of my actions when I lean down and kiss Finn in that dark corner. Their body melts into mine in a way that I can only hope is in agreement with my actions. In that dark corner we were no longer in public, no longer in the mess of bodies that were thrashing around us, we were just two people in love.

Chapter Eighteen

I wake up the next morning to my phone exploding with messages. I decide the best course of action is to check the band group chat first. It was also the first thing that popped up on my phone screen after I turned my alarm off.

♪♪undead stars♪♪

MARI

have you guys seen this?

[photo]

people on the internet are saying it's finn and kyle. Is that true?

I freeze as I see the picture. It's blurry, but I can clearly make out my hair and crop top behind Finn's mess of curls. In that dark party someone snapped a picture of us kissing and probably used it to make some money off us. And sure, maybe it was irresponsible of Finn and I to be going to a party and making out in a dark corner, but we didn't think anyone had even realized we were at the party, let alone decided to take a picture of us in such a compromising position.

♪♫undead stars♪♫

HARPER

how can they even tell that with that angle?

it's probably just hopeful fans

STEVIE

what is that?

finn? Kyle? I need answers.

do you just like making my job hard?

how am I supposed to do damage control when you go out doing that

kyle and finn I will be up to your room in twenty minutes if I don't hear something

KYLE

shit

STEVIE

is that all you're going to say Fishman?

im going to need you to start explaining yourself

Stevie is pissed. Of course she is. But if this is how she finds out about Finn and I, we've just fucked up. Big time. She was not supposed to find out like this. She already hates me enough as is and this is just going to make things worse for the both of us. I know it is.

I look up from my phone and over to Finn who seems just as glued to theirs. My heart breaks seeing them looking so panicked as they grip their phone tighter than I had ever seen them hold it.

"This is bad." They say when they look up and meet my gaze. And I know they're right. This is not how any of this was supposed to happen. But now we're going to have to go out and talk about our relationship publicly. And not even just publicly, but we're going to have to talk about it with Stevie, their ex.

"How are you so sure of that? Maybe we can turn this into a positive thing?" I hated how hesitant I sounded as I tried to reassure both Finn and me. And I know I'm not handling it well. I have over two hundred texts blowing up my phone. I can't help but imagine who they could be from.

"I don't know! But this is so bad."

"Finn. Baby. Now we don't have to keep hiding. It could be worse." I try to console them and look for the positives, but I keep thinking about what my dad is probably saying in my texts and I can't pull my thoughts away

"But are you ready for that? I barely feel ready to be on tour with like, real fans." They look down at their phone again and tears begin to fill their eyes.

"Finn, baby, you're not alone. I'm right here with you. I promise. We are going to figure this out. Together." I pull their phone from their hands and put it down on the bed.

. . .

♪♪undead stars♪♪

I throw my phone to the side and look towards Finn. The panic on their face evident. In all the years I've known them, I've never seen them get as anxious and worked up over anything.

I sit on the bed next to Finn and pull their hands into mine. "Baby, I need you to talk to me. What's going on? What's got you so worked up? This side of you is all new to me, tell me what I can do and how I can help. We are in this together for as long as you'll have me. But for this to work I'm going to need you to let me in."

They nod, squeezing my hand, and my heart breaks as I watch them struggle so evidently. "I guess there's a lot I've been keeping from you, and the rest of the band too I guess, but I think that's a good place to start."

"Just start wherever you feel the most comfortable."

"Everything's just happened so fast, I guess. I mean, I knew we were posting online, obviously, but I never actually expected it to take off and then all of a sudden there were all these eyes on me. On us, I guess, and I think it just came with this pressure to portray the person that everyone else wants me to be. I mean, up until a few weeks ago I was the token queer band member. And like this is all so cool and I'm so grateful for all of it, but some of the things people have been saying about me, about us, online has just really been getting to me recently. It sounds so stupid when I say it out loud, I know they're strangers and mean nothing, but people can be really mean when they hide behind a screen."

"Oh sweetheart," I say, rushing to hold Finn close. "I know the people online are awful. And I know this is scary. This is a whole lot of information that we're putting out into the world. But I can promise you it will be okay. We will be okay. Whatever happens next, I'll be right there. I'm not going anywhere. I know you're scared, and I am too, but no matter what we've got each other and we can control the narrative. The choice to make our relationship public was taken from us, but we can choose how we move forward."

Finn looks at me and my heart breaks even more. They are just trying to take in everything I was saying and find a way to be okay with all of it in two minutes before we head down to face the rest of the band.

Stevie looks angry when we emerge from the elevator to find the rest of the band waiting for us in the lobby. She doesn't say a word to any of us as we walk to the restaurant in the hotel. She only looks back at us once and she doesn't look happy when she does so.

I can't even begin to imagine what is going through her mind right now. Everything is blowing up in all of our faces. She's got to be so insanely angry right now. And not even just at the situation, but the fact that Finn and I have been together right under her nose. Especially after the way they ended things with her.

We all sit at the table. I have Finn to my left and Mari to my right. Harper and Aspen are sitting across the table from us with Stevie. She just glares at Finn and I as we pick up our menus, perusing them to avoid eye contact and collect ourselves. My hand comfortably lands on Finn's thigh underneath the table. I try to rub soothing circles into the exposed skin. I can just feel them buzzing with anxiety. Anyone with a pulse in our general area can feel it.

Eventually a waitress comes by to take our orders and Finn and I can't hide behind the menus any longer.

"Finn. Kyle. One of you better start talking right now or we're going to have a problem," Stevie says with a stern look on her face. Finn shrinks in their seat next to me and I grab their hand knowing they need the extra support.

"I'll start," I say, feeling Finn deflate and relax beside me. Stevie just raises an eyebrow at me urging me to continue. "So, we started dating not too long ago. We wanted to keep it as something private between the two of us, well, because it's a pretty intimate thing. I don't think we should have to explain why we chose to keep our relationship between the two of us, but we did. And we went out for pride and ended up at a party and I know I was drunk," Stevie's glare hardens, "I don't know about Finn, but I'd assume we both were actually, and we kissed at a party. So what? Finn can speak for themself, but I really like them. Like a lot. And I want to see where this goes."

Finn looks up at me with a look I can't quite discern as a smile begins to spread across their face.

"I know we can't control the reactions to this news. And it is pretty big news for the fans I guess, but I think we're both pretty serious about this. At least I know I am. I don't know what damage control you think you have to do, but maybe we leave it for now. The pictures are us, but it's hard to tell. On stage Finn and I can maybe try to play it up a bit, and let the fans speculate. We don't have to tell them. At least not yet. If anything, that should draw in the fans. Keep them talking about us. And I know I don't know much about any of what you're doing, Stevie, but I don't see how that would be a bad thing."

Stevie looked between the two of us, contemplating for a second before speaking. "Okay. That's actually not a shitty idea." She smiles.

"Damn, I thought that was a pretty good idea. I'll take not shitty I guess., I say with a smile.

"As long as all of you are on the same page with this. We play into the ambiguity of the situation and draw attention."

"Fine. If that's how you want to play it, go for it. The three of us will have a meeting about this later," Stevie says, her glare never leaving Finn. "We need to talk. But for the rest of you, no more days off until the album is done. We're only on tour for another week and you've barely got half an album put together."

"Yeah I'm not doing that." Finn mumbles so only I can hear.

"That's a lot of pressure," Aspen speaks up nervously,

talking about working on the album. "We maybe have one more song that's ready to record, but to write and record like seven more in a week is a big ask."

"Other artists can get it done much faster," Stevie says coldly.

"I get that, but all five of us have to be happy with everything. It just takes more time." Harper says, jumping to Aspen's defense.

"Well maybe you all should be working harder then. Every second of downtime should be going to the album."

"That's impossible. We need to eat and sleep and use the bathroom. Are you really asking us to work on the album while we take a shit?" Mari asks, cracking a smile.

"You don't have to be a smart ass. You know what I mean. You're going to work hard. All of you."

"Can't we just push the deadline back? I thought that was an option if it ended up being too much?" I say, but with the way Stevie's already upset with me, I'm definitely not the person to be speaking up about it.

Stevie just rolls her eyes at me. "We'll see, but try your best to get it done. All of you."

♬

Before our show that night, we have an interview with a local news outlet. I am sat right next to Finn, which is a smart idea considering we want to try and play up our relationship. Even if it's just how we would end up anyways. After Stevie confirms that the camera can't see our hands, I hold Finn's in mine and play with the rings on their fingers throughout the interview.

The interview was what was to be expected for us at

this point. The questions were all variations of the same. That was until the picture was brought to our attention. The interviewer held up a copy and asked Finn and I outright if it was us saying: "The internet is convinced this is a picture of the two of you at a pride party the other night. What do you have to say to that?"

I leaned in, squinting my eyes as if I'm really trying to figure out if that could in fact be us in the photo.

"In this photo that you posted to your Instagram story of the two of you, Kyle, you are wearing a top that looks just like what the redhead in the picture is wearing." She clearly wants us to admit something. To give her something that will draw attention to this very interview. But this is just the start of the one thing we were working on.

"The shirt does look similar I guess, but I don't know. It's a pretty popular top, and we did get home pretty early that night. And that photo is just so blurry it's hard to tell. You can't even make out a clear face."

She sighs, realizing she isn't going to get from us what she really wants. "So, are you saying this isn't the two of you?"

"There were just a lot of people and a lot of parties. And you can't even see the face of the other person. How do you know it's not a woman?" I cringe as the words come out of my mouth and Finn stiffens next to me. I know immediately I've hit on some nerve, and I feel bad. I spoke without thinking, and by the way they immediately drop my hand I know I've messed up. Finn doesn't deserve that kind of a comment on their appearance, blurry or not. "And besides, I'm not into women anyway. So, if that is a woman, it can't be me. That could even be lesbians for all I know. The picture's just not clear enough." I try my best to say something to clean up the mess I've created, but it's too late. I've stepped in the shit and am going to have to deal with the consequences of my thoughtless actions.

The interviewer nods, realizing that this is the best she was going to get out of us. I can only hope that I said enough to patch over my screw up. The interviewer then decides it is in her best interest, and ours, to move on and ask other questions regarding the album we are working on among other things and well, that was something that we were better equipped to talk about at length.

Finn and I walk into our dressing room together after the interview. I reach for them, trying to grab their hand and hold them close. I'm feeling on top of the world. Our relationship was both public and private at the same time in a way that I was honestly not too mad about. But then they pull away, busying themself with literally anything else. It is almost as if they are just trying to do whatever isn't spending time with me.

The interview had been hard. I had to give them that. All interviews are hard in one way or another, and this one was no exception. And they just look so tired. I try to give them space for a little while. With a few hours between now and the show itself, time to decompress might not be such a bad thing. Even if Stevie thinks we should spend every waking minute of free time we have working on this damn album.

I put my headphones on and pull out my laptop, deciding to take a listen to everything we have recorded so far. After spending so much time in the studio, there is a lot of material. I had mixed and produced the music that we'd put out prior to the tour, and while we occasionally have professionals work on it, something we've learned is that it's just cheaper if I do it. And I'm not terrible at it. I also really like it.

I get to work on our first song. Listening to everything together and messing around with it a bit. I don't want to do too much to the song, after all, I want all of us to shine as best as we can, but playing around with it a little bit can't hurt. And the more I work on it the more I begin to realize we sound good. Really good. And honestly that feels pretty awesome.

When I finally look up from my laptop, Finn is deeply engrossed in their phone, no doubt looking though social media comments. They have this focused look to their face and I can't help but snap a quick picture. I open my phone to post it to my Instagram story, only to see that they had posted one of me, hard at work. I meet their eyes and start laughing as I post my picture.

I get up and make my way over to where they are sitting in the small room, coming up behind them and wrapping my arms around their neck. "Hi baby," I whisper in their ear, and I just love the way it sends shivers down their spine as I linger there.

"We need to talk, princess," Finn says with a more serious look than I have ever seen from them.

I pull back, stricken, and look at them with a mix of confusion and concern written across my face. "Is every-thing okay?"

"Everything is fine. I just need to get something off of my chest otherwise it'll never be addressed." I'm starting to get more nervous. What had I done?

"Did I do something?" I feel stupid the second I ask this dumb question. I know what I did. I know what I said.

I just hadn't wanted to bring it up and remind Finn of what I had done. But clearly there had been damage done.

"Not intentionally, princess, but I just need to make sure this doesn't happen again."

I nodded. "This has to do with the interview, doesn't it?" I ask having a pretty good idea of where this conversation was going as I finally start to piece it together.

"Oh. Wow, yeah actually. You might be more self-aware than I thought, princess." Finn smiles at me in that teasing way I have grown to love. "We're going to be talking about that picture for a while, probably for the rest of the tour, as we try to capitalize off of whatever we think this relationship might be turning into. And I'm having a lot of fun teasing this relationship without explicitly stating anything, it's really entertaining, but can we just not make comments about me looking like a woman in those photos? Like, I get that it's easy. It's probably the easiest thing to point at in saying that can't be us, but…"

Their voice trails off as they try to search for words. "Baby, you don't need to explain. You're not comfortable with it. You don't want to be referred to in that way, I understand. You are setting a boundary within reason, and I'd be an ass not to respect it. And I'm sorry I said that."

"Princess, thank you, but please let me explain." They reached out and grabbed my hand. "You've only ever known me as Finn or Finnley, as trans, as nonbinary, as me as I am now, but early middle school me was a whole different person. I was a little girl hurting and longing to be the person I am today. It's been so long, and at this point it's so easy to forget who I once was, but that becomes a glaring reminder and hurts. I know I just have more feminine features. I love them, but there's so much more to me than that and I know you see that too."I squeeze their hand tightly as they look at me with a look I can't quite discern. "I just don't know if I want to make that part of my life public. Not yet at least. I know it could help so many people. I know there are so many fans that could benefit from my openness, but I want to do it on my own terms."

"And you deserve to, baby. No one is going to force you out if you're not ready. And I know I wasn't there during those rough years, but if you think I'm going to let anything happen to you, you'd be sorely mistaken. I will be more careful. You know I don't always think before I speak, but I could benefit from doing that more often. I'll try to do it more. You deserve that."

I move to sit on the couch in the little dressing room and they curl up right next to me, resting their head on my shoulder. We sit like that for a while before the door flies open.

"Five minutes bitches!" Mari calls into the room, leaving the door wide open as she leaves. I look to Finn with a smile and we both pull on our outfits for the evening, taking care to touch up our makeup before we head out on stage.

Chapter Nineteen

We go out on stage to a roaring crowd. It is honestly magical. If I had thought the energy any other night was amazing, this show topped that in an instant. The energy is wild, on a whole other level. We play the first song in our set, and I am honestly surprised to hear people screaming along to the lyrics. Sure, at every show there's a handful of people at the front, but it's nothing like this. The fans are just electric. I bounce around the stage during that first song and it truly feels amazing. I can't say I played perfectly, I never do, but if I did mess up during that song I didn't even notice.

We get to that first bridge and I bounce over to the drums, vibing with Finn as they play in a way I don't even know how to describe. As we round out the end of the bridge we get to my favorite part of the beginning of the show.

"New Orleans we are the Undead Stars!" Harper calls out into her microphone to screams from the audience. "Are you ready to have some fun tonight?" The fans' screams are deafening. "If you know the words, and I know you do, I want to hear you sing along!" And that's our cue. I look to Finn and Mari and Aspen and with a nod we start to build up to the final chorus.

As the screams die down at the end of the song, I step up to my microphone and look to Harper. "Welcome!" I say into the microphone, eliciting a few more cheers. "As was just mentioned, for those of you who don't know us, we are The Undead Stars!" More cheers. "And I think it's about time we introduce ourselves, how does that sound?" Screams and cheers echo throughout the room and I think I hear someone scream out an "I love you, Kyle!"

"I guess we should start front and center with our beautiful and talented lead singer Harper!" The applause is unreal. "And that cute little blonde on keys is Aspen!" I call out and I think, for the briefest of seconds I see Harper blush as Aspen does a little improv. "And we can't forget my badass bestie on the bass Mari!" Mari does a fun little bass solo that rivals no other and then I turn and look back at Finn and wink before saying into the microphone "and that sexy drummer back there, that's Finn!" The screams are the loudest I've heard yet, and I can't help smiling to myself knowing what I did.

"And we can't forget our resident heartthrob and guitarist Kyle!" Finn says as I play my little guitar solo, blushing in surprise. Normally it's Harper who introduces me, but I guess this is all just part of our plan.

Harper jumps in to introduce our next song and I can't help but look back at Finn with a look of both shock and wonderment. They give me a sweet little smile and a wink and then we're off. I clearly wasn't paying attention,, but I didn't realize Finn had counted us in and the song was supposed to start with just guitar and drums. Apparently, I just spaced and didn't realize Finn had started.

"Dude!" Mari shouts at me as she ran over to where I was just standing dumbfounded. "It's your part! Play!" I turn bright red and then start to play, my fingers finding their place on autopilot. I look out at the audience and honestly, I'm relieved to see that it doesn't seem like anyone in the audience realized I had messed up. They probably just assumed that it was all part of the way we performed the song. At least I'd have that.

When the song comes to an end, I am relieved. This is a part of the show where Harper and Aspen talk and banter a bit. They've been having really cute banter on stage and it's pretty fun to watch, normally. It's really just how we get to the next song. While they are bantering, I step away from my microphone and make my way over to Finn.

"How bad was that?" I ask quiet enough that no one in the audience would hear.

"Not bad at all, princess. You're fine. We should be the only ones that noticed," Finn replies leaning away from their microphone.

"Warn me before you go on introducing me like that. I know we've been joking about the heartthrob thing but, damn, that really threw me off." I laugh.

"Oh, I could tell, princess. Maybe warn me before you call me sexy to a sold-out audience."

"Okay, yeah that's fair, baby, I'll warn you right now that I'm going to be keeping that up." I wink at them as I turned to head back over to where I was supposed to be standing.

"Oh good, the two of you are done having your little moment." Mari says into her microphone as I turn around.

I stop in my tracks and go bright red at that comment. "Want to let the rest of us in on whatever this is?" Mari gestures between Finn and I.

"I just had a little question." I say into my microphone. "Nothing more than that. We got it taken care of."

"Sure…" Mari says with a smile and there are a few scattered cheers and whistles from the fans that were in the know. I just roll my eyes. "Well now that you're done with whatever that was, I guess we can go ahead and play the next song." She smirks and Finn counts us in for the next song.

For the next few songs, I stay rooted to my spot right in front of my microphone, not straying too far from it. If I was to turn away at all, I'd end up missing something else and I'd already had enough embarrassing mishaps for one show. I'm not looking to add any more to the list.

However, in deciding to play up the potential for a relationship between Finn and I, we decided to add in the unreleased song and have me introduce it.

"So, we're going to be trying something new for you all today," I say into my microphone as it came time for the song on the setlist. "As I'm sure some of you are aware from our social media activity lately, during our time off on this tour we've been working very hard on an album." Cheers erupt from the audience.

"Tonight, we wanted to test out a new song for you. It will be on the album when it comes out, eventually, and we might even add it to the setlist permanently depending on how tonight goes. But how does that sound? Do you want to hear a brand-new unreleased song, New Orleans?" I call out to the audience who couldn't have been more excited.

"Good. I'm glad, because we're playing it tonight regardless." I laugh into the microphone. "But for a little background, I wrote this one with the help of Finn for someone really special to me and it means the world to get to play it for you tonight. This is Summer Sunsets."

We start playing the song, and honestly that was probably one of the best ideas that anyone in this band has had for intrigue. I could just imagine what the videos of us playing it would be like. Especially once the fans get a hold of the fact that Finn and I wrote what is essentially a love song together.

Playing this up just comes naturally to me. Honestly, I wouldn't have had it any other way. Getting to play the song Finn and I wrote together, for each other, for an audience for the first time was a wild experience. I find myself hanging back on the stage closer to where Finn is sitting, playing the fun guitar riffs we wrote together right to them. I can't help but have the feeling that the fans are eating all of it up, and I couldn't have been happier. It is everything I wanted it to be and more. I am getting to play the song I wrote for my partner to my partner, with my partner. The whole thing is a cool and wild experience unlike anything I have experienced before.

We come off the stage to Stevie with an expression I can't quite read. She looks to Finn and I and looks somewhere between proud and angry. Or maybe it was a combination of both, I can't be too sure. But I walk right up to her, knowing that I am probably going to get in trouble for what happened early on.

"Kyle. Finn. I need to talk to both of you. The rest of you can go pack up your dressing room. Or stay. I don't really care what you do, just be quiet."

I look to Finn and for the first time I'm sure what way this will go. Normally, if Stevie is pulling any of us aside after a show like this it's because we messed up in one way or another and she's going to give us a stern talking to. But the smile on her face today said otherwise and while I did mess up, twice technically, I know she still wants to talk about this morning.

"Kyle, you messed up quite a bit tonight. I'm surprised. You normally don't fumble that much. Not in one show. But each time you kept feeding into the rumors. I'm not okay with it by any means, but you did a good job with that part. The talking with Finn I wasn't too happy about, but it did give a cute moment and when you look on your socials later, I'm sure you'll be tagged in a whole bunch of posts. But missing the intro, we need to talk about that. Can you tell me what happened there?"

I sighed. "No one told me Finn was going to introduce me tonight."

"I'm not sure I'm following," Stevie says with her brows furrowed.

"Finn introduced me as our resident heartthrob."

"Yes. I heard that. I have ears. I was sitting right here."

"They were clearly flirting with me! I wasn't expecting it, and it made me feel some kind of way." I look at my lap embarrassed with having to admit that to Stevie.

"Okay, but you called me sexy in front of everyone," Finn says getting defensive.

"Baby, I wasn't blaming you." I said, forgetting for a minute that Stevie was in the room with us.

"Get a room!" Mari called from the corner she was sitting in, scrolling on her phone.

"Okay, I think I understand now. Maybe keep doing it.

Or don't if it's going to be too much of a distraction. After looking at social media for just a minute, and we'll see more tomorrow about what the internet is making of Summer Sunsets, but I think it might be a permanent addition to the setlist. I'll let y'all know tomorrow if it's a permanent change."

I nod as her expression gets even more stern, if that is even possible.

"We also really need to talk." Stevie directs her comment to Finn "I just have to say, I am a bit surprised. Especially since you, Finnley, won't even talk to me after all those letters I've been leaving you."

"What letters?" Finn asks, completely confused.

"Well, you weren't talking to me in person, and you weren't answering my texts so I figured I'd leave you letters in your dressing rooms or hotel rooms whenever I had the chance to just get in there before you. Did you really not see any of them?"

"I really didn't." They sigh and turn to me. "Did you?"

"No," I say too quickly, and too high pitched for anyone to actually believe me.

"Kyle," they say in the tone you would use to scold a child. "Did you see any of these letters?"

"Yeah. I did. I know I shouldn't have read the first one, but I know Stevie's handwriting and I was intrigued. When I read it she was asking you to take her back and you had just been so hurt by her and honestly she was awful to you, no offense, and I've had this crush on you for years and not to be all like 'you were now single and I saw it as my chance,' but you were and I did and you're just so much happier now too so it all worked out in the end. And after I took the first one and hid it from you, I just kept doing it and then we started getting closer and got together and I figured it just worked out for the best." I ramble on trying to defend my actions but knowing I'm only digging myself into a deeper hole.

The room goes eerily quiet, and everyone turns to me. Phones have been put down, conversations have gone dead, and every single person in the room, whether or not they are part of the band is staring at me.

"Dude what the fuck!" Stevie's the first to speak and she's nearly shaking with rage, but nothing beats how red and angry Finn looks.

"Kyle, you did not have the right to make that decision for me. You don't get to just decide what's best for me."

"I was only trying to help you." I know I thought I was doing what was best, but I've made a mistake, and I've lost this battle.

"No, you weren't. You were selfishly trying to keep me away from her and all for yourself. You didn't have my best intentions at heart. You never did. You just wanted her out of the picture so you could live your little fairytale. Well guess what? This fairytale of yours is over. We're done." They storm off, leaving me standing there dumbfounded. Mari shoots me a glare before running after Finn while I just stand there, unsure of what to do next.

Chapter Twenty

Checking my phone directly after waking up the next morning proved to be more of a mistake than I had initially expected. Or maybe I should just be getting used to this. The fans on our social media pages are just wilder than I had even thought was possible. Pictures and videos from the show are all over my social media feed. It seems almost as if everyone on the internet is talking about Finn and me. Of course they are. And every single comment I read makes me want to crawl into a hole and die there. I had something so good, and I had to go and screw it all up.

After scrolling for a few minutes, I decide to put my phone down and get out of bed. Finn is sleeping in the bed next to me, but they won't even talk to me. They won't even look at me. And I hate it.

With a show in the evening, we are spending most of the day in the studio again. I wish I could say I was bored of it, but honestly that would be a total lie. Honestly, I've been enjoying the time we've been spending in the studio.

However, I'm not looking forward to the long drive that would precede the studio time. I'm also not looking forward to having to write songs with Finn. How are we supposed to write together if they won't even look at me?

I stumble into the bathroom after another fifteen minutes or so to brush my teeth and start getting ready for the long day ahead of us. Finn comes in after a few minutes before realizing I'm there and leaving abruptly

"Your phone's ringing." They say after a few minutes, sounding annoyed. I sigh as I pick up my phone, seeing it's my dad calling. *Of course it's my dad calling.* That's just what I need right now, a phone call from my dad. I put it down on the counter and answer the phone, putting it on speaker.

"Hi dad. What do you need?" I say as I finish brushing my teeth.

"I can't just call my son?" he replies and all I can do is take a deep breath.

"At eight in the morning? You're on your way to work. You wouldn't just call if you don't have a lot of time. But that really doesn't matter. I'm running late. What do you need?" I don't want to be having this conversation. Not now anyways. But I know it's going to happen eventually so I might as well get it over with.

"The whole internet seems to be going crazy over some pictures that may or may not be of my son kissing another boy, I have a right to check in on those grounds." And there it is. The one thing that he would be calling me about.

"Right. So are you concerned about me, or just concerned about how it'll make you look having a gay son. And for the millionth time, Finn is nonbinary."

"I'm trying to run damage control over here, kid." Right. Damage control. Not caring for his son and how hard it might be for me to have this picture circulating and the whole world speculating as to whether or not the picture is of me.

"Yeah? That's what you care about?"

"Do you know how it looks for me to have a gay son?" And here we go, back to this argument again.

"Sorry dad, wasn't really thinking about your image when my phone was blowing up over something that I was trying to keep private," I snap, not wanting to deal with this for a minute longer.

"So that is a picture of you?" If he says that one more time I might just explode. How can he just make something that is so scary for me all about him? How can he just not care at all? Actually, that's a lie, he does care, just not about me, about his image and how I'm making him look being gay and out and just trying to be myself.

"Yes, Dad. Those are pictures of me," I say, resigned.

"You could have at least given me a heads up. This has been a nightmare at the office." Do people in his office actually care or is he just saying that to make me feel guilty? If he is, it's not working. The only thing I feel guilty about is messing everything up with Finn. I've destroyed the one good relationship I've had in ages after having pictures of us taken without our consent and then leaked and the only thing my dad can care about is his image?

"If I knew this was coming, I would have. I would have liked to tell you and mom about my relationship myself and not have you find out through social media like this. But here we are. Not that it matters anyway since we broke up last night, not that I expect you to care." I mumble the last part and know he doesn't hear it as he keeps bull-dozing over me.

"And the things that have been posted about you, those clips from your show last night. Kyle what the hell do you think you're doing?" He's not asking if I'm okay, how I'm doing, if the pictures are freaking me out, nothing.

"Capitalizing off of these unfortunate circumstances. Or at least we were trying to. It's been giving us pretty good publicity."

"So that's what you're calling it now."

"I can call it whatever I want." I'm so fucking fed up with him I want to scream.

"You should be refuting the rumors."

"No."

"What do you mean *no?*"

"I mean no. Dad, the rumors were true, but Finn and I wanted to keep this as something that was at least a little more private. And playing into it is making us money. It's drawing people to us, increasing streaming of our music, getting people talking. But it doesn't fucking matter anyway since we broke up and now can just go back to how things were."

"But that's just the problem. People are talking. Your mother is really upset about this."

"Is she now?"

"Don't use that tone with me, kid."

"If she really was, why hasn't she called me?"

"Kyle Alexander, take that back right now. You know she just doesn't want to bother you."

I huff out a laugh. He's just trying to make me feel bad. And I do, just not about what he wants. "She's probably just worried about how I'm holding up with all of this newfound attention. Again. Just like she was when the band first went viral. She's probably scared and worried for me, and all you care about is how it will be received at work. That's a really great way to just tell me you aren't proud of me. Thanks dad. I really need to go. I'm going to be late. We've got one more show and then I'll be home and working with you for the rest of the summer just as you want. Okay?"

"Just call your mother. Please."

I roll my eyes knowing I will probably end up calling her anyway. "Okay, Dad. I'll call her." I throw my phone down onto the bed and just sit there for a few minutes. I should have expected this. I should have been waiting by the phone for his call.

I call my mom, and it confirms my suspicions. She was just concerned about me, like any good parent should be. She sounds appalled at the way my dad handled everything but is glad to know I'll be home soon, and we'll be able to get through this together.

♬

In the studio the next day, Finn and I sit as far apart from each other as we possibly can and it's making the writing process difficult for the rest of the band. But if I'm being honest, I couldn't care less. I know that's awful, and I get it, but how am I supposed to sit in this room and work on all these cutesy love songs with Finn when they won't even look at me?

I keep to myself in a corner for the entirety of the studio session. I do feel shitty for it. We're all just trying to do a job and trying to keep Stevie off our backs and churn out a whole bunch of songs in one afternoon before we have to get on stage tonight and finish out this tour. It's not easy for any of us.

As everyone else is working on songs together, I'm sitting in my little corner with my notebook out and guitar on my lap trying to figure out how to fix the mess I've gotten myself into. I've royally fucked up with Finn, and I know I need to make it right. Now I get how Stevie felt when Finn wasn't talking to her. It now makes sense why she would do anything she possibly could to get them to even just look at her. *I wish they would just look at me.*

I start fumbling around on my guitar, deciding that if I'm not going to be working with the group I might as well write something else. I start writing an apology to Finn in song form. It's as close as I'll get to actually being able to apologize to them right now, and maybe if they hear it and they understand where I was coming from, they could forgive me. I doubt we'll end up using any of what I'm writing, I'm not a great songwriter, but there could be something good here. Maybe.

And it's not like I think this song is going to solve everything. I'll be lucky if it even gets them to look at me after all this, but there might just be a way that it could work.

I fumble around with chords, trying to find a key and chord progression that has just a hint of melancholy to it. Something that is just slightly somber in its entirety. I try to stick to minor chords for that effect and go on my phone to look up other songs with melancholic chord progressions to see how other artists have achieved something similar. I read through a few articles before coming to one that I really like the song of. I mess around with where on the guitar I'm playing it, and the key I'm playing it in until I have something that I think sounds pretty nice.

I know focusing on the words rather than on the key of the song and the chord progression should be where I'm starting when it comes to writing this song for Finn, but I just can't help myself from wanting to start with the one part of songwriting I'm confident in.

I play around with different patterns of how I want to play the chords, messing around with different sequences and different structures, noting it down in my notebook and then, for good measure, I record a quick voice memo.

When I look to the rest of the band to see what they're doing or if they have even noticed my absence from the rest of the group, it seems like no one really does, so I just keep going. They're all so engrossed in the song they are working on it seems like they don't even notice I'm not working with them. They don't even notice my absence. Is this how the last week of tour is going to be? Are we really about to end on a note where Finn can't even look at me? Did I just fuck up everything?

I continue to work on my song, starting to just write a bunch of ideas and phrases out onto the page, though I feel like I have no idea what I'm doing. I've never written a song before on my own like this. I've only ever written in group sessions and in those sessions, I've been focused so much on the instrumental aspect of the songs that I don't know if I can even write a song. Am I just going to make a fool of myself? Will it even be good?

When I was writing with Finn, they would often take the things that I would say, random words and phrases that would just come out of my mouth as we were talking about the subject matter and arrange and rearrange them until those phrases or random words became lyrics. But all I can keep writing is "I'm sorry" and "I fucked up" and "I know I hurt you" but I know that is just not enough. Nothing I can write will be able to convey just how heartbroken I am. Nothing I write will be good enough.

But maybe that's just it. I don't have the words to say how sorry I am. I don't have the talent to write a song that says everything perfectly, I just have to be able to say it.

I stare at my notebook, and I know that whatever this song is, is not going to be something I can do alone, and not going to be something that I'm going to be able to finish before the end of tour. But maybe that's what I need. Maybe I need to give it some time, give Finn some time, and find a way to approach this that is real and authentic. Taking time away can be a good thing, I guess.

After a half hour or so, Harper gets up and comes over to where I'm sitting and trying my best to write something.

"And what are you working on over here?" she asks gently as she sits down on the floor next to me taking a look at my notebook.

"Making things right. At least for the sake of the band," I whisper not wanting Finn or really anyone else to hear me. "What were you working on over there?"

"Heartbreak, mostly. Finn is really hurt, you know."

I swallow thickly, not wanting to cry in the middle of a studio session.

"Yeah. I really fucked up. I don't know how I'm going to fix this. Writing them a song seems so silly. But like, maybe if I can use the band as a way to get them to listen to it, it will be worth it?"

"You did fuck up, I'm not going to lie to you there, but you do need to try and fix this, at least for the sake of the band. We're not going to be able to stay a band if the two of you aren't talking to each other." As Harper says that I feel my heart drop. The five of us spent all of high school working so hard to get to this point and I could have just fucked it up for everyone by being stupid.

"I'd quit before we get to that point. I love all of you too much to hurt you like that. It's my fault we're in this situation. If it gets to that point, I'll quit. Find another guitarist and keep going."

Harper looks at me with tears shining in her eyes at the thought. "How about we just not let it get there so we don't have to worry about that. It's your band too."

"Do you really think this could work?" I ask, wanting the honest truth even if it might not be what I want to hear.

"It depends on how you deliver it. I think if you show up on their doorstep in California with your guitar and play them the song it might actually work in your favor, but you'd actually have to get there and with college move in for all of us right around the corner, I don't know how you're going to make that happen. But right now, I think they need time. Whatever you're working shouldn't be finished before tour is over. Or, at the very least, if it is, just hold onto it for a little longer."

"For Finn, for this band, I will find a way. I know I just have to make this right."

Chapter Twenty-One

Our final show goes about as smoothly as I expected it to. I try to keep to myself and do the one thing I know I'm good at, but even that is a struggle.

Getting through the first few numbers is increasingly hard as the show goes on. Everything is running smoothly, at least from an outside perspective. And everything looks like it's running smoothly on our end too, but every single time I look towards the back of the stage and see Finn sitting there with their head down trying to just get through the show, it breaks my heart. This is our *last show of the tour*. We should be celebrating and having fun and feeling sad it's over, not struggling to even look at each other.

When we get to Summer Sunsets on the setlist, I have to introduce it. "This next song is a new song for our upcoming album," I say to cheers from the audience who seem so excited to hear the song. "It is a song that I worked very hard on and one that means a lot to me. I wrote it with the help of a person who means the world to me, and I know they're not all that happy with me right now, but I want to make things right and I will work as hard as I possibly can to fix things." I look back to Finn for a second. "I know this song isn't out yet, but if you know the words, sing along."

The song starts and it takes everything in me not to start crying on stage. I can't imagine what my dad would have to say if he saw that. I'm sure it would be something about how I'm not a real man and how real men don't cry and all that bullshit that I just wish he would stop saying. So, I keep it together. I can cry later. I can cry when I'm alone in my room tomorrow night.

Considering Finn and I are not talking, the show runs incredibly smoothly. But even as we rush offstage and into our dressing rooms to pack up, they brush past me and refuse to even look me in the eye. It hurts. It hurts so badly, but I know I deserve it. I know I got myself into this situation and I'm going to have to get myself out of it.

We don't even get to celebrate the success of the tour. Well, we do. Stevie and our label throw us a little party after the show, but I can't enjoy it. I try to stick to myself in a little corner again. I don't want to ruin the night for Finn who seems to be having a good time. I don't want to mess things up more than I already have. I've done enough damage.

Harper keeps looking over towards me every so often, and while I know she wants to come over and include me in the fun, we both know it's best if I keep to myself. So that's what I do. At least with the way Summer Sunsets has been popping off, the label isn't too upset about us having to push back the album deadline. They can see how hard we were working on it, and with five people all trying to work on one project it just moves slower, and I think they understand that.

The next morning my alarm goes off bright and early, and I do my best to silence it immediately to not wake up Finn. I consider leaving them a note on the hotel notepad, but even a stupid hotel notepad feels like it holds too much meaning and weight, so I don't. I just leave as they continue to sleep.

I meet Mari in the lobby and, after we get our instruments and other equipment out of the van and say goodbye to Stevie, we call an uber and head to the airport. The rest of the band is staying out in California, lucky them, while the two of us are heading back east and heading home. I don't want to be going home. I want more than anything to be staying in California with Finn and Harper and Aspen and to be going to college in California to study music and feel like what I'm doing is going to actually be useful for me. But I know that's just not possible Not without my parents' singing off on it. Not without getting my dad to agree. And he may never actually let me do anything I would want to do.

Traveling with two guitars and a summer's worth of clothes isn't easy. While Mari has two suitcases to my single one, I have two instruments to her single one. And we both have backpacks and other carry-on items to make the six-hour flight back home as easy as possible.

When we board the plane, I sit in my aisle seat and while I might want to sleep, I decide to pull out my notebook and work on the song I'm writing for Finn. It's hard to really work on a song while up in the air in a public space where I don't really have the space to be singing different lyrics as I try to find the melody for the song. I go to the bathroom at least three times with my phone to quietly sing different versions of what I'm working on to be able to hear them back and see if any of them work.

But after an hour of that, and an hour of getting strange looks from the people around me, probably out of concern for my bowels, I decide to stay parked in my seat and just focus on the lyrics. I can worry about cadence and melody later.

I struggle through writing the lyrics, but by the time the plane lands I'm at a pretty good place. I have bits and pieces of a verse or two and maybe half of a chorus, but I'm struggling to actually write the words without having the melody behind me to help me out.

Eventually my mind drifts away from the song. We spent all summer on this tour working our asses off on an album that's just not done yet. We're so close to being done, but now the time crunch feels more intense. Mari is leaving for Europe in just a few weeks and then we're all starting college not long after. How are we all going to be able to work on music together when we're all in different little corners of the world?

The plane lands and I reluctantly get off and make my way through the winding airport to the baggage claim where Perri and Aubrey are eagerly waiting for me.

"Welcome home!" Perri exclaims, wrapping me in a giant hug. "We've missed you all summer." I smile at her, and then turn to give Aubrey a hug too.

"I've missed y'all too," I say with a sigh as I stare at the baggage carousel waiting for the bags to start coming out. I just want to get home.

After what feels like forever my bags finally make their way out onto the carousel and into our hands.

"I don't understand how you have so much stuff," Perri says with a huff as she loads my suitcase into the trunk of her car. "I didn't even think you owned this much."

"I may have picked up a thing or two while on tour," I say sheepishly.

"A thing or two? How much had you packed to begin with if this is close to what you had?"

"I don't know. I was gone for a few months, though! I had to be prepared for anything and everything."

"Including dating your drummer?" Perri fixes me with a stare as I climb into the car.

"Yeah, but that didn't last long."

"Dude! How'd you manage to fuck that up?"

"Can we talk about it tomorrow? I'll give you all of the details, but I don't want to get into it before having to go deal with my parents."

"So, we are hanging out tomorrow?" Aubrey asks as we merge on the highway.

"Did you have other plans? I mean it's still the weekend and I don't have to start working for my dad until Monday."

"No, I just," she looks to Perri, and I could see them having some kind of silent conversation. "Thought you'd want to spend time with Perri alone."

"What made you think that?" Does my best friend really think I'd rather spend time alone with my cousin, her girlfriend, when I could spend time with both of them? She looks to Perri again, and it starts to make me nervous. "Okay, what aren't you telling me? There's clearly something going on. Spill."

"It's not a big deal, why are we making this a big deal?" Perri says, the comment directed at Aubrey.

"It is a big deal, and we can't keep it from him forever." Aubrey sighs, grabbing Perri's hand.

"You're starting to scare me, can you please let me know what's going on?"

"It's nothing bad. Seriously, babe, just tell him."

"Fine. If it's just so important, I'll tell him." Perri sighs. "When we get home."

"Babe, seriously?"

"Yes. I'm completely serious. I want to be able to look at him when I tell him this. Not drop the bomb on him when I can't even see his reaction."

"There's a bomb? Is this like bad news or something? You're starting to scare me."

"It's nothing big, just about our living situation for the fall."

"What do you mean? The three of us are going to be in that really cute suite together, right? Just like we planned. Right?"

"Well, we may have gotten a really cute one-bedroom apartment for the two of us right by school... and that might have thrown you into the random housing selection and we should have told you we were planning on doing that, but you weren't here and then it just happened, and we're really sorry," Aubrey says in a panicked ramble.

"We're still going to be at the same school and see each other all the time. We're just not going to live together," Perri says in an attempt to make me feel better, but the damage has already been done. My own cousin and my own best friend don't want to live with me. The only good thing about going to this goddamn school and now I just have to be okay with it. But I'm not okay with any of it. Maybe there's still time to transfer.

"No, it's fine," I say trying to keep the peace. "We'll still see each other all the time and maybe even take that science class together." They exchange a look that has me thinking we won't be taking the class together, but at this point I could care less. I just want out. Of all of it.

Aubrey shakes her head and sighs. We sit in silence for the rest of the drive, music playing softly through the speakers.

Aubrey and Perri help me carry all of my bags, and two guitars, into the house when we pull up into my driveway. I'm not sure I want to go inside. Actually, I know I don't want to go inside. I want to be anywhere else but my parents' house. Even after a few months away, I'm still not ready to face my dad, let alone start working with him on Monday, but here we are. I'll have to walk into the house at some point. At least now I'll have my friends with me as a buffer.

I unlock the door and walk into the house with Perri and Aubrey trailing right behind me. I barely walk into the kitchen before I see my parents sitting on the couch waiting. They both stand up as they hear me come in with my girls.

"Hi, Mom," I say softly as she pulls me into a hug. I really had missed her. I think it was just so easy for me to not miss her when missing her also meant missing my dad, but in reality I missed her so much. I say hi to my dad too and give him an awkward hug before dragging the girls up to my room.

"Well, that wasn't awkward at all," Perri deadpans as she sits on my perfectly made bed. My mom must have been trying to make sure everything was perfect for me coming home, even though I was only going to be home for a few weeks at most.

"Yeah, things with my dad have been tense since I left for tour." I sigh as I flop down onto my bed next to Perri. "I've been wearing nail polish." If it was anyone else, that comment wouldn't have made an ounce of sense, but with Perri who has literally known me and my parents my whole life, she knows exactly what I'm saying. And Aubrey, having been around long enough now, does too.

"No shit. I think the entire world knows that." Perri rolls her eyes. "So what the hell happened with Finn?"

"I thought we were going to wait until tomorrow to talk about that," I say trying to change the subject.

"Kyle Alexander Fishman, tell us what the hell you did," Perri says with a teasing tone in her voice and a concerned look spread across her face.

"Why do you assume it's my fault?"

"Because we know you. And we know they didn't do anything."

"Are you so sure about that?"

"Wait, did they actually do something?" Aubrey asks, concern flashing over her features as well.

"No. It was me. I fucked up."

"I knew it!" Perri yells with a triumphant smile.

"Jeez you don't have to be so excited about my failures."

"Sorry. I'm not. I was just right. You know I like being right." Perri tries to hide her smile, but I can see it clear as day.

"Our manager, and their ex, was sort of leaving them these little love letters in our hotel rooms and dressing rooms and I just kept getting to them first and y'all know how bad my crush on them has been for years. So, I hid the letters. And of course they found out. And now they're really mad at me and won't talk to me and I get it but it really sucks."

"Damn, that's bad. Even for you."

"What's that supposed to mean?"

"Aren't you like used to fucking up everything good that comes your way?"

"Um, no."

"Weird. Thought you were. Whatever. So, what are you going to do about this because holy shit you need to fix this if you want to stay with your band."

"Damn you're really coming for blood. You think I don't know that? It's fucking scary. I don't know exactly what I'm going to be doing, but I'm currently writing a song and maybe we'll get it to them under the guise of using it for the album since we couldn't seem to finish that. And maybe if I'm lucky I can fly out to them and actually talk to them about it. But that's if I'm lucky."

"Damn, so you really fucked up."

"It's bad. I'm aware."

"You really need to fix this. Like, *really* need to fix it."

"I know. I'm just having such a hard time with this song. I am so not a songwriter it's not even funny. I need all the help I can get."

"Kyle, are you asking us for help? Do you want our help?"

"If you want to, I don't want to pressure you into anything you don't want to do. I mean, we will be spending a fair bit of time together. And I could use an outside opinion at the very least," I say nervously, not wanting to look either Perri or Aubrey in the eye knowing how badly I need this to work.

"Of course we'd love to help! We just want you to be happy," Aubrey replies with a smile before Perri can even get a word in. "We've probably got a few ideas that can help."

"And maybe if we help, you'll pay for our ice cream tomorrow?" Perri says, genuinely asking for the bribe even though I probably would've done it anyways, just happy to be back with my best friends.

"I will do whatever it takes for your help. I'm desperate."

"Clearly. Remind me that I should be taking advantage of your desperation more often."

"Perri!" Aubrey scolds.

"What? He's making himself an easy target." Perri says matter of factly.

"If bribing you is the only way I'll get you to spend time with me, it will be worth it. You know I love spending time with you," I say with a bright smile, doing whatever I need to be able to get through.

Even after Perri and Aubrey leave I stay hidden in my room, trying my best to just avoid my parents at all costs. It's not that I don't want to spend time with them. Correction, it's not that I don't want to spend time with my mom, I just can't handle another minute with my dad. Not right now. Maybe in the morning I'll be more equipped to handle it, but right now I'm most certainly not equipped to handle anything of this nature. I will deal with my parents in the morning with a clearer head and more energy to be berated by my dad.

Chapter Twenty-Two

The next morning, I stumble down the stairs, still exhausted, for breakfast with my parents before heading to Perri's. I walk down the stairs to the smell of bacon and eggs. My mom has already put a huge stack of pancakes right in the middle of the table, and my dad is sitting there, clearly expecting me to go join them. I look to the garage door, wishing I could just walk right past them and get in my car, but I know I'll have to sit with my parents, at least for a little bit.

"I made your favorite breakfast," Mom says with a hopeful smile andI sit down at the table right in my usual seat.

"Thanks Mom," I reply with a smile as I begin to fill my plate with a few pancakes, covering them in syrup as she joins my dad and I at the table with the bacon and an egg for me, sunny side up just how she knows I like them.

"So, I don't know about your father, but I want to hear all about your tour. You've been gone for the past two months and I can't help but be a little curious about where you've been and what you've been up to." My mom smiles, so wide and inviting I can't say no to her.

"Tour was amazing. It was so cool getting to travel to all those different cities. I didn't even realize how much of a reach we really had as a band. I guess with everything so focused on social media it's easy to just see numbers as numbers and not real people with lives and opinions. And they're some really cool people too. We sold out almost every night. That was the coolest part I think. We're getting close to four hundred thousand followers, which is wild, and we really only got to see a glimpse of that." I beam, so proud of myself and my band.

"How big were the venues you were playing?" My mom asks, clearly intrigued by the tour while my father just sits at the table, disinterested. Not that I expected him to care, but he could at least pretend to take an interest in what I'm doing. He could at least *try*.

"Most were upwards of a thousand people, but some of the bigger venues I think got up to fifteen hundred, so the venues were pretty small, but for our first tour that's still pretty big."

"Sounds like it," Mom says with a proud smile. "I'm so proud of you, you do know that, right?"

"Yeah mom, I do. Thank you." I look to my dad who won't even look up from his plate. I guess if you don't have anything nice to say don't say anything at all, but I would love for him to say something.

"We both are," she says looking to my dad for his input, but he stays stoic.

"So, what was so important in your free time that you couldn't be doing work for me?" he asks and that is most definitely not what I had been expecting from him.Of course the only thing he would care about after I spent months away from home was why I couldn't spend time working for him and being his little puppet.

"A lot of different things actually. We spent a lot of time in the van driving from city to city, and we had shows back to back, I didn't really have wifi or even access to good service during those drives. And then before we had to be at the venues, we would sometimes be doing interviews, in between working on an album. We've been trying to write it and arrange it together for the most part, so we spent a lot of time in different studios across the country writing and recording. And now I'm focusing on the production of the album in my free time. Our label wanted us to finish writing, recording, and producing an entire album while we were on tour. So that did eat up a lot of our time. Not that we were able to finish it."

"And why are you doing that?" He doesn't even seem slightly interested or proud of all I have accomplished, he just wants to see how it will fit into his long term plan for me. I shouldn't be surprised.

"I really like doing it. It's really fun for me. I'm not great at the songwriting part so getting to spend the time working on the other aspects of creating the album is the thing I can contribute." I don't understand why I have to defend my choice to produce this album for my band, or even just work on it in general, but I can see that it's just not a skill he thinks is going to be useful for me in the career he expects me to pursue.

He looks at my mom and though I can't quite discern the look he is giving her, the look she returns is one of annoyance.

"You really shouldn't be doing that. Especially once

you get to school. It's fine now, I guess, since it is the summer, but when it gets to the fall, I don't want you doing that anymore. You're going to need to focus on your schoolwork. A business degree is hard, especially at your school. I did it thirty-five years ago and it was tough then, I can only assume now it's much harder than it was when I did it. You are going to have to keep that in mind."

I haven't been home for twenty-four hours and all he wants to do is remind me of how important it is that I do exactly what he wants for me. He needs me following his plan so I can be successful and any other way I try to be successful just won't work.

"I am, Dad. I still don't understand why I can't go and get a music business degree. I understand you want me to get a practical degree and go to your alma mater. I get that. But I will be learning a lot of the same things, just with a music focus. I don't think that could hurt. Especially as things with my band are really taking off. I do think that's going to be something I'm able to pursue full-time after college. We all are planning to. I think this tour really showed us how possible it is for us to make the band our lives."

"Kyle…"

"I get you having some twisted need for me to go to the same school you did, but have you ever really sat down and considered what I might want for my own life? Instead of trying to make me a mini you, why can't you just let me be whoever I want to be? What is so hard about that?" I snap and I feel all of the anger and frustration I've been feeling over the past few years, but especially the past few months, bubbling to the surface and I don't know if I can keep it in any longer.

"Kyle..." My mom says this time, a hint of warning in her voice. I'm only going to make him mad. We both know that. Hell, all of us know that. But I can't help myself. I've sat around and taken his bullshit for far too long. I've let him trample over me and every aspect of my life, trying to shape it to be just what he wants it to be, and I'm done being not good enough. Because with him I never will be.

"What am I missing here? Because, in all honesty, I would love to go study music business in LA. It would put me much closer to the rest of my bandmates as we continue to work towards finishing this album and put me in a much better place geographically for music. I understand you wanting me to have a practical degree. But why can't we compromise on this? I don't get it. All I've done my entire life is work to be the son you want me to be, but clearly, I will never be enough for you, so I might as well just live my own damn life and be happy instead of making myself miserable trying to please you. I am not your do over. You don't get to decide how I'm going to live my life so I can fix all of the mistakes you made with your own. I am my own fucking person, and I will make my own decisions."

Every ounce of composure I have leaves my body as I yell at my dad. I can't keep living in his image while also trying to pursue my dreams. I can't do everything, and if my dreams are actually coming true, that's the path I need to follow.

My dad's face is red with anger. Maybe I messed up, but all I really did was speak my mind and finally tell my parents how I really feel about having to follow the plan they've set out for me.

"You know, I don't think this has anything to do with

business or even the music," my dad says calmly, almost too calmly. "I think this has everything to do with that boy you've been kissing."

"You mean Finn, who is nonbinary by the way, and the drummer in my band."

"So, you are dating him."

"Them, Dad, and I was but I screwed it all up right before the tour ended. So we're actually not together anymore." I take a deep breath to keep myself from crying. Of course he would find a way to blame this on my feelings for Finn and on me being more openly and outwardly gay.

"You were so fine going with the plan we had so carefully laid out for you until we let you go on this tour. Maybe I shouldn't have been so lax with you this summer. It's given you the wrong ideas. You're going around publicly kissing boys and thinking you can study whatever you want. I raised you better than this."

I look to my mom, pleading, she returns my gaze with a sad smile. I take a sip of water to calm myself, willing myself not to cry. "Dad, when are you going to realize that this is my life? Not a second chance for you to do yours." I try to remain calm as I speak, but my voice wavers and I can feel the tears building.

But that was the wrong thing for me to say. I know it the second the words come out of my mouth, but it is too late. He is furious and I am determined to stand my ground. "I'm sorry? Can you please repeat yourself? I'm not sure I understand what it is you're trying to say because no son of mine would be so blatantly disrespectful."

"I've worked so hard on this band, it's been like my

passion project for all of high school, and it's starting to take off. I just want to see where it goes. Why can't we agree to have working for you be my backup plan? If things with the band don't work out, I can always come back home and work for you and then you win. But can I at least go out and try to live this life that I want for myself instead of the one you're forcing me into? I hate to say it, but the life you want for me just sounds miserable. It's not what I want.." I put my fork down as I wait for his response. We are at some kind standoff.

"Sweetheart, you've made some really good points," my mom says with a hopeful smile and for once I think she might actually be on my side. "Why don't you give your father and I some time to talk this over. Just give him some time to process everything you've just said and let us work it out together. Okay?"

"Yeah," I say with a relieved sigh, "but for the record, Dad, I'm gay. I've always been gay and always will be. You can hate it all you want, but it's always going to be part of who I am. And I'm really happy. I'm really happy with who I am. I know asking for your support is a big ask, but it would mean a lot to me."

He looks at me with a cloudy expression and I just get up and head to my car. I sit there for a bit and just stare out into space before driving over to my cousin's. I know my parents want what's best for me. They always have. They don't want to hurt me. I know that much. I've always known that. And while I know my dad just wants to set me up for success and follow in his footsteps, he just needs to take a step back and see that it's not what I want or need for my life.

I know deep down he doesn't want to hurt me, and

maybe he's scared of my potential failure and just wants to make sure my future is secure. But is a secure future, a boring one at that, worth the pain that he's causing me? Is it worth all of this mess? I don't think it is. I think if he could just see what this band is becoming and see for himself the upward trajectory we're on, he'd see that this isn't some crapshoot that might not work out. Our entire tour was sold out. And we're only getting bigger. And sure the next four years might make things a bit slower for us, it will make creating music and touring just a bit harder and will probably mean we'll have to work twice as hard to be able to keep up with the rest of the industry, but once that's over and we graduate and we all move to the same city and are able to pursue this full-time, nothing is going to be able to stop us. I have so much faith in us and our ability to one day be topping the charts.

As a band, we got lucky. We had a viral moment which turned into a record deal and an EP, which we had already been working on, and then in the blink of an eye we were touring. It's crazy how fast this has all happened and we all know college is going to slow that down. But when Finn and I were doing our little flirty thing onstage and in interviews, it was gaining so much traction. Being talked about on social media, and even a few headlines, has been wild. And I don't think I can let my parents stop me anymore. If I have to find some other way to move out to California and pay for college I will, because I can't do this anymore. I just wish I was making more from our music. I don't care what they say or what they want from me. I'm doing this my way whether they like it or not. I'm going to make it happen.

I drive to Perri's once I've calmed down and arrive

within five minutes. It's been so nice having my favorite cousin living so close now that she's moved.

I walk up to her front door with my guitar in hand and am greeted by my aunt who is just as thrilled to see me as Perri and Aubrey are. I head up to her room, following the familiar hallways until I'm standing in her doorway.

"Oh my god! I thought you were supposed to be here almost two hours ago. What the hell took you so long?" Perri says from where she's lying on her bed barely even looking up at me.

"Sorry. Breakfast with my parents was a nightmare. I might have blown up at my dad. But it's fine. I kind of just did it and left. And now I'm here. Ready to keep working on this song for Finn."

"So, you actually want our help with this. You weren't lying?" Aubrey asks nervously.

"Yeah. Did you actually think I was lying? I really do need help."

"I just don't get why you're asking us for help. We know nothing about writing songs," Perri says as I pull my guitar out.

"That's why I'm asking for your help. You'll tell me if it all sounds like shit and then I can maybe call Harper, and we can work it out a bit more."

"Asking for our help is a mistake. I hope you know that."

"I'm more just asking for you to be in the room with me while I write the song so I can bounce ideas off of y'all if I'm having trouble," I say, knowing sometimes the best way to work something out when I'm stuck is to just talk it through with someone.

"If that will help, we can be your sounding board. We just want to help you get back together with Finn."

"Me too. If I can't at least get them to forgive me, I might have just screamed at my dad for nothing."

"What do you mean?"

"If they don't forgive me, the next logical step is going to be for me to quit the band."

"I don't get how you got there, but okay."

"Well, I'm the one that fucked up. If anyone is going to quit over this shit, it's going to be me because we know damn well working together when they won't even look at me is a recipe for disaster."

"I guess you're right about that. But there's not another way for you to just get to a place where you can exist together?"

"Maybe, but right now they won't even look at me and I hate it so much. I wish I had just shown them the first letter when it first came and let them talk it out with her instead of taking matters into my own hands and deciding that they shouldn't even see the letters."

"Dude, you didn't make them fall for you. You do know that right? What you did was take away the option to go back to a shitty relationship."

"I get that. But I did it so they would be with me. I thought if they didn't get back with Stevie I would have a chance. And then when I got that chance, I blew it."

"You did totally fuck it up. Why didn't you come to us when the note showed up in the first place? We could have talked some sense into you and told you not to keep it from them. We would have told you how stupid you were being."

"I know. I know you would have. But they've been

flirting with me for years, like since we met almost, and I thought I finally had my one opening to actually step in and finally show them that I was interested too, and I completely blew it. What the hell am I thinking? How is a song supposed to just fix this?"

"Music is what brought you together. It's what will keep you together for years to come. Don't forget that. And you're already prepared for the worst-case scenario. Now come on, write the damn song."

Chapter Twenty-Three

That night, probably because they felt bad, my parents decided to take me out to dinner. Maybe it was because they know I would never make a scene at a restaurant. Especially not now with the band blowing up and the potential that it ends up online. I could never do that to my bandmates. The press we got from Finn and I kissing was stressful enough and that wasn't actually bad press. If we were to get real bad press, like if one of us were to do something awful publicly, it could ruin us.

My parents also decided to take me to my favorite restaurant for dinner which is a great way for them to tell me that I'm probably not going to like whatever they have to say. But maybe I'm just overreacting and they're taking me to my favorite restaurant because it's been two months since I've been home, and they want to have a sort of welcome home dinner.

After a short but awkward car ride where no one actually says anything, we get to the restaurant and are ushered to a booth in a secluded corner. At least maybe we'll be kept away from prying eyes while we have what is likely to be a very intense, private family discussion.

As we walk to the table, we get stopped by a young girl and her mother. The girl looks nervous, almost scared, and her mother has the sweetest smile on her face.

"I'm so sorry to bother you, but my daughter was wondering if you're Kyle from that band she loves. What's it called again sweetheart?" the mother says, looking to her daughter and urging her to speak.

"The Undead Stars," her daughter says in a whisper.

"I am," I say with a smile. I've only gotten recognized out in public a few times and never by someone so young. "What's your name?" I ask her as I crouch down to be more on her level.

"Sophia," she says softly.

"That's a beautiful name," I say. "Do you have a favorite one of our songs?" She looks to her mother, silently begging her to answer for her.

"Sophia's favorite song is Cosmic, isn't it?" Sophia nods and I look around for a napkin and a pen.

"Sophia, would you like to take a picture with me?" I ask and it feels a bit odd to be asking if she wants a picture. The thought alone that someone would want to take a picture with me because of the band is weird enough, and asking always makes me uncomfortable, but I can tell that this small fan isn't going to ask me herself.

She nods and I pull her in for a hug as we snap a few pictures. Someone comes over with a napkin and a pen and I scrawl a quick and totally cliché *follow your dreams* onto the napkin and then sign it before handing it back to her. We say our goodbyes and my parents and I make our way over to our table.

Once we're left at the table, I pick up my menu as if I don't know what I'm going to get just so I don't have to look at either of my parents who have decided to both sit across from me. Nothing makes this feel more like we're about to have a serious talk than them both staring me down as I peruse the menu I know like the back of my hand.

"So, we just wanted to talk to you about what you said this morning," my mom says softly. I put my menu down and look across the table at my parents. My dad is looking down at his folded hands, letting my mom take the reins for this conversation.

"I just want to start by saying we both love you very much and we never want to put you in a position where you are made to feel otherwise," she continues, and I take a sip of my water as I brace for whatever's about to come. "But that being said, while we understand why the conversation this morning went down in the way it did, you could have handled it better. I know in the heat of the moment emotions were high, but that doesn't excuse the way you attacked your father."

I nod as I feel my body go into a sort of dissociative state, one I've used for my parents time and time again, where I just disconnect from everything they're saying and the situation as a whole and just nod and say yes until we can move on from the situation so that I can make it out in one piece. Sometimes that's all I can do.

"But that's not what we want to talk to you about. At least not right now. And maybe we should punish you for that, but you are an adult and about to go off to college and we have to treat you as such. You had a lot to say about your future and what you want and after talking things over with your father, we've decided that you should be able to study whatever you want at whatever school you want to be at."

I'm in complete and utter shock as my mom says those words. I never thought we'd ever get to the place where I'd be completely allowed to go off and do what I actually want to do. I thought I'd forever have to try and force myself to fit into their mold while trying to find ways to do the things I love just as I always have. I never in a million years thought I would be given this kind of freedom.

"You're joking right?" Is the only thing that seems to be able to come out of my mouth. This dinner was supposed to be an hour or two of my dad telling me how selfish and ungrateful I am and how he's worked so hard for me to get all the opportunities he's given me and that he even moved our family across the country, and moved away from our extended family so he could be able to provide certain opportunities for me only for me not to take them.

I look to my dad and for the first time he looks up and his eyes meet mine and we both freeze.

"Your mother and I just want you to be happy. We never wanted to hurt you or make you feel like we didn't support you," he says, and it looks like it's painful for him to say. He keeps averting his eyes and then looking back to me. "It seems I've done a lot of that lately."

"Dad, I know you mean well, and you always just want what's best for me, but you're so stuck on what you think is best for me that you've completely ignored what I want. And I'm not saying this to be mean. I just can't keep fighting for your approval and fighting to be happy because lately those have been two completely different things, even down to painting my nails and wearing makeup onstage. I've just been doing what makes me happy. I can have this fabulous night and feel incredible in my outfit and the makeup and all of it and then I get offstage, post a few pictures online, and then I hear from you and I hate to say it, but the excitement is ruined and I just feel like shit."

"I never wanted you to feel like that. I was only trying to look out for you and protect you. People out in the real world are cruel. They are hurtful and say hurtful things, especially about people like you, and I just don't want you to be subjected to that."

"I get that dad, I do, but what you're doing isn't protecting me from those people and the things they might say, you're being one of them. I'm not saying this to upset you, that's the last thing I want, but if we're being completely honest here, I can take the hate messages from strangers. Those don't bother me because they are just people hiding behind a screen who I will probably never meet. But when it comes from you, that's when it hurts because you are my dad and I just want you to be proud of me."

"Son, I am so proud of you. I need you to know that. And watching you earlier, interacting with that little girl who listens to your music, I think it just made me realize how incredible you really are. Your mother and I have watched you work so hard on your music and your craft, and now you have actual fans who want to come see you and support you and who want to come up to you in public and ask for a picture and I just don't think I realized how serious this was for you."

"It is really serious. A record deal is really serious. And

we've got a pretty good one at that. And I really want to pursue this, if I didn't fuck everything up."

"Don't tell me we're finally okay with this, and you've gone and messed it all up."

"It should be fine, but Finn's kind of sort of not talking to me right now."

"Sweetheart, how did that happen?"

"I may have done something really stupid and now they kind of hate me and I'm trying to fix it but I don't know how without traveling back to California to be with the rest of my band, well really just Harper and Aspen. But I'm starting work with Dad on Monday and have to worry about getting ready for college and moving and all of that."

"Screw working with me on Monday. You clearly don't want to do that, and it's not going to serve you well at all. What will serve you well is flying to California and trying to fix this, and after how awful I've been to you, I think I can arrange for that," my dad says, to my shock. "And while we talk about arranging for big changes moving forward, why don't you reach out to those colleges in California that you got into and really wanted to go to and see if it's too late for you to start in the fall."

"Are you serious? You're going to pay for me to fly across the country to try and fix this and you want me to see if I can go to one of the schools in California?"

"Like I said, we just want you to be happy, and if that's what's going to make you happy then so be it. We'll make it happen."

When we get home that evening, I rush up to my room and immediately text Harper and Aspen and let them know what my plan is and to see if they can help at all.

Then I start emailing the admissions offices of the three schools that I got accepted to in California, one of them being my top school, to see if it's not too late for me to transfer.

While texting Harper and Aspen, I pull out my guitar and my notebook and start working through the song again, until it's well past midnight and my parents have booked me a flight for the next morning out to California. I send a crappy voice memo recording of what I've got, the chord progression, melody, and lyrics that I'm still not happy with, and hope that the two of them can come up with something to fix the mess of a song.

Chapter Twenty-Four

I land around noon, California time, and am greeted by an excited Harper at the airport. We're both eager to get working on the song and despite how tired I am after only getting about three hours of solid sleep, I'm wired.

She drives us straight to a local studio where Aspen is waiting for us. I immediately get comfortable on the floor while Harper and Aspen get to work on my lyrics. I record the different guitar parts I want to use for the song and upload them to my computer and start messing around with what could potentially be used for the other instruments when it comes to the song and putting together a sort of demo, minus the vocals, to send off to everyone so that when we all go to record at different times in different places we are able to kind of know what it is that we need to record.

"Kyle, we can never let you write a song alone again. How did you even write a song this bad?" Harper teases as she goes over my lyrics with Aspen.

"Are they really that bad?" I ask, genuinely worried

that I've actually written something awful. "I mean, I know I'm not great at songwriting, but I didn't think my lyrics were that bad."

"They're not good," Aspen says.

"When I was writing with Finn I would just like say things and then they would turn whatever I was saying about whatever we were writing a song about into lyrics so I was trying to do that I guess, but the only thing I could think of was I'm sorry and I really fucked up."

"And there lies the issue, my friend, you need to dig deeper. What are you really feeling? And don't go giving me all that surface level bullshit. I need the deep shit," Harper says sternly.

"I don't know." I sigh, putting my guitar down and laying on the ground.

"You do. They're not talking to you. They won't even look at you. This song isn't just about your guilt and how you want to make things right."

"What do you mean?"

"It's so much deeper than that. It's about your feelings and how much you love them and how much it's hurting that you know you fucked up and ruined everything. It's about how it hurts to see them so hurt and knowing you are the cause of their pain, and how you know so deeply who they are as a person and maybe used that to manipulate the situation to get the outcome you wanted."

"But isn't the whole thing supposed to be an I'm sorry I fucked up vibe?"

"On the surface, yes, but they need to really hear how much you care and how much you hate that you messed this up."

"So, like, I need to write about how I'm willing to quit

the band and give all of this up, give up everything I love, if they truly never want to talk to me ever again because I would rather let them live out their dreams than ruin it for them?" I say, knowing it's just going to be best to put every single feeling out there. Maybe that's why the song itself has been so bad. I've been trying to just say I'm sorry in a song where I need to show how sorry I am, and how I would ruin my whole world if it meant they were happy.

"Exactly! There it is!" Harper exclaims excitedly.

"Wait, you're not actually considering quitting, are you?" Aspen asks, concerned.

"If we can't work this out, yeah. I would."

Aspen looks like she's about to cry and honestly I feel like I'm about to cry too. I don't want to give up this band that I've worked so hard for. I don't want to have to walk away from the songs that I've poured my soul into. I don't want to leave these people who have been more of a family to me at times than my own family. But if it means they will be happy and not have to be stuck working with me, it will be worth it. I will do whatever I need to in order to make sure they're happy.

"I might have an idea for a lyric and maybe it's awful and you totally don't have to use it because we've already established, I'm bad at this, but what about *I would ruin my whole life if it meant you were happy?*" I suggest nervously.

"That's actually not bad." Harper says, not even looking up from my notebook which she's taken over. "It actually fits really well right at the end of the chorus. We did need one more line." She sings out the entirety of the chorus using the melody I had written for it with completely new words, ending with the line I just wrote, and it feels and sounds so much better than what I had written.

"I really like that," I say, sitting up.

"Yeah. I feel like that's the message of the whole song. That's what you want to say to them. You want to say that you feel so guilty that you would ruin your whole life and give up everything. That's what the song's supposed to be."

Harper and Aspen go back and forth a bit more over different lyrics tweaking things until they feel the lyrics are perfect. I look them over and read through them a handful of times, trying my best to commit them to memory.

We then finish up recording the demo and I know I'm going to listen to it a million times before I end up going over to Finn's new apartment tomorrow and surprising them by singing it for them. The whole thing, the whole idea of just showing up uninvited and hoping for the best feels so scary.

"Do you really think this is going to work?" I ask nervously as I fumble around with my guitar, not yet wanting to pack up and head over to Finn's to do the damn thing.

"I think there's a chance. I mean the two of you did get brought together by music." Harper says trying to be reassuring, but I know we're all unsure of if this will actually work or if this is just going to blow up in our faces. "And besides wasn't Summer Sunsets how you two admitted your feelings for each other?"

"I guess it was in a weird way. I guess when they started writing it, and I saw what they were writing, I realized my feelings might not be one sided, but still, this feels so different, it's not like I'm working on this with them to tell them how I feel."

"Well, you can't really do that if they're not talking to you," Aspen says matter of factly.

"Anyway, I'm sending the demo over to Stevie and Mari to try and get them on board," Harper says, not even looking up from her phone.

"And you think that's going to work? You think all of this is going to work?"

"Kyle, this could end really poorly and completely blow up in your face, but you won't know if you don't try."

I nod and start to pack up my guitar. I guess Harper is right. I won't know if this is going to work without going through with our plan and making it happen. But if I fail, I could lose the band. All through high school I had two things that were keeping me sane, my friendship with Aubrey and our other friend Taylor, and this band. And when Aubrey was going through hell after her sister died and I couldn't go to her with my own shit, I turned to the band. I could spend hours with her just being there and supporting her through whatever she needed and then I would walk into rehearsal and the second I walked into that classroom it felt like a weight had been lifted off of my shoulders and I would be okay. That's all I could really ask for. And now I've gone and screwed up the best part of the band, my relationship with Finn, and if I can't fix it, I will lose everything.

I know if this goes poorly, I will be okay. I'm learning how to be a better songwriter and I'm making good connections now to be able to go off and work on my own music if I need to. Or maybe I will go to college and make some really amazing friends in the music department and then we'll start a band and with my decent sized following I could get that to pop off.

But how would my leaving affect the rest of the band and their success? This upward trajectory we're on feels momentous and unlike anything we ever will experience, but could my leaving ruin everything? I don't want to come across as self-centered or self-absorbed in even considering this, but a lot of the press the band has gained recently has been through my relationship with Finn and the speculation behind it. If I leave and that chapter is truly over, would people lose interest? Part of the whole appeal of us as a band, I think, is that we have been friends since middle school and created an insanely exclusive club at our school to keep this between the five of us and give us a rehearsal space. I just don't want to do anything to hurt my friends, Finn included, obviously. So, this can't fail. I need to make this work.

I'm pulled from my thoughts as my phone buzzes with an email from one of the schools I had reached out to about transferring, my top choice school.

Dear Kyle,

Thank you so much for reaching out to us regarding your desire to join us in the fall. As much as I would love to get you set up with an academic advisor and get you started in the enrollment process, I won't be able to offer that at the moment.

My heart sinks as I read the start of the email. I know I should keep reading, but this was the school I wanted more than anything. I don't know what I had been thinking even reaching out so close to the start of the semester. There's no way any of the schools are going to let me just start in the fall. I continue reading.

Unfortunately, at this time, with the semester starting in a matter of days and a full roster of incoming freshmen it is just not something we are able to offer. But after revisiting your application that you sent in back in the fall, I would like to offer you a spring semester start if that would work for you.

I'm attaching a document that should go over everything we will need from you to be able to enroll you in the spring. The only issue with enrolling so late is that we won't have space for you in our dorms. I can recommend a few apartment complexes that are close to campus if you need help finding one.

I'm looking forward to seeing you in the spring.

I can't believe my eyes as I read the rest of the email. So, I can't start in the fall. That's okay, I guess. I don't think I've even looked into communicating with the school that I'm supposed to be attending in the fall as to my change of heart. I could still start there in the spring, if my credits would transfer, so I won't fall behind. I'm going to make this work and I'm going to get on the right path towards pursuing my dreams. I'm going to be okay.

"How has she already listened to it?" Harper says,

pulling me out of my thoughts as she flashes her phone screen towards me to show Mari calling. "You have notes already?" Harper asks as she answers her phone.

"Damn I miss you bitches!" Mari exclaims as her face pops up on Harper's phone.

"I'm assuming you listened to the song and have notes?" Harper says with a no-nonsense tone.

"What makes you think that?"

"You never call me, for starters. But also, I sent that song off to you maybe ten minutes ago."

"What's the deal with the song? And why is Kyle in California? I'm completely missing half of what's going on here. Someone please explain what the hell is going on?" Mari sounds impatient.

Harper fills Mari in on the basics of what's going on with me showing up in California to her satisfaction.

"So, the song then," Mari says once she's been all caught up.

"Is Kyle's attempt to make up with Finn."

"You know them better than the rest of us," I say hoping my nervousness doesn't come through in my voice. "Do you think this is going to work?"

"I don't know. I know they're really fucking hurt and heartbroken. Dude, they really fucking trusted you. You really fucked up."

"I know. I know. I want to make things right. I want to fix this."

"Then I think this is your best shot. If they're even going to consider forgiving you, this is the one thing that could actually get them to think about it."

"You really think so?"

"Look, music is everything they care about. I can't

think of a time when they haven't been writing songs or working on a song. They've always got something going on in their mind, some string of lyrics that they're working through. That's just who they are. And I think we all know how hard songwriting has been for you. Words are not your strong suit. And I say that with love. I think it will mean a lot to them to see that you really pushed yourself out of your comfort zone to write something for them. I also think they'll have some notes on some of the phrasing. Even I have a couple notes, but we can worry about that later. It's not the main focus of this right now. So, go! Get your ass to their apartment and make things right with them! We're all begging you!"

I laugh as I finish packing up my guitar and the backpack I brought with me. I'm going to fix this as best I can. And to do that I've got to leave this damn studio.

Chapter Twenty-Five

The twenty minute drive from the studio to Finn's apartment is agonizing at best. I sit in the backseat while Harper drives with Aspen in the passenger's seat and I can't even just enjoy the scenery as we drive. It's not like the drive is scenic by any means, but this is the city that I've always wanted to live in. This is the one place I've always wanted to be. There's been nothing I've wanted more for as long as I can remember and if this doesn't go well, I could lose all of this.

Sure, that might be a bit extreme. Come the spring, I will be going to college here. I will get to spend four years calling this city home, and that feels like such a dream come true. But half of that dream was spending the time here with the band and one day getting to live in a house or apartment as a group, which sounds insane, but little fourteen-year-old me thought it would be the coolest thing getting to be roommates with my band-mates who I love more than life itself. But now, I guess it seems ridiculous to think that the five of us would want to live in a house together. I think we'd end up killing each other.

But the dream of getting to work together for the rest of our lives is still going strong. And that's the dream I've wanted to pursue above anything else. And I'm so goddamn close. So insanely close, I can taste it.

We park a few blocks away from the building Finn's living in. Harper and Aspen have already been to Finn's apartment a few times and have been helping them move in while I've been sitting on the outside for the past few days, wishing I could be in this beautiful city with my friends.

They walk me to the apartment and hit the buzzer. Finn, clearly not expecting anyone, is slightly confused but after hearing Harper's voice lets us in. And by us, I mean me. I know heading up to their apartment alone when they're expecting Harper might not be the best look, but I know for a fact if they knew I was here I wouldn't make it past the door.

"Just take the stairs up to the third floor and then make a left. They're in 3G. It's not going to be hard to miss," Harper whispers as she sends me in, as if they could hear us from all the way down here.

I walk up the stairs to the third floor, the floor they're living on, with my acoustic guitar on, my hands shaking the whole time. I follow Harper's directions and before I know it, I'm standing in front of their door.

I stare at the door for a minute before knocking. This is the last moment where I don't know how they're going to react and the last moment before everything changes, whether for good or bad, only time will tell.

I take a deep breath, willing my hands to stop shaking

and my pits to stop sweating. Why am I sweating so much? It's just Finn. Finn who I've known and loved since middle school. Finn who I've had a crush on for years. Finn whose heart I shattered into a million pieces.

I wipe my sweaty palms on my jeans and knock again

"I thought I told you to text me before you come over and not just show up unannounced. I could've been out," Finn says as they come to the door expecting Harper only to freeze when they see me. "Kyle. What the fuck are you doing here?"

"Look I know you hate me. I hate me. What I did to you was beyond horrible, and I feel so fucking bad. I want to fix this. And I know nothing I say will undo all the pain I've caused you, but with the help of the girls and some really hard conversations with my parents, I've written you a song and I'm here and you don't have to forgive me. You can hate me for the rest of our lives, but please just let me play you the song. All I'm asking for is five minutes of your time and then I will leave and if you want me to, I'll never come back, and you will never have to see me again."

"Kyle, you can come in. And maybe breathe for a minute and collect yourself. I can grab you a water if you'd like," they say as they move aside to let me in, and I just shoot them a confused look. Why are they being so nice to me? They shouldn't be being so nice to me. They should be hurt and upset and yelling not letting me in and getting me water.

"Uh, yeah, sure," I say nervously as I follow them inside. Now that I'm here there really is no going back, and I have to do this. I have to make this right. I have to fix this. Finn comes back into the room, and I smile nervously at them before wiping my sweaty palms on my jeans once again. They put the water down on the coffee table for me and shoot me a shy smile. It has me thinking that this could go well. I hope it goes well. But at least they are open to whatever it is that I'm trying to do here. They cross the room and sit on a chair while I take a seat on their couch.

I take one last deep breath, close my eyes, and start playing the song. I keep my eyes closed for the duration of the time I'm playing for them. Even when I want to, I know I can't open my eyes to look at them. I know I won't be able to handle however they're looking at me.

I get through the first verse smoothly despite my hands still shaking and as I build momentum in the chorus, I find myself starting to get choked up. I didn't think this was going to be so hard. I didn't think it was going to hurt so bad.

As I sing the last line of the chorus for the final time, the last line of the song, the last time I sing the words *I would ruin my whole life if it meant you were happy*, I finally open my eyes and look over at Finn. They have tears streaming down their cheeks and I can't help but match their tears with my own.

They get up and walk across the room to come sit next to me, and I can't help the fear that creeps into my mind. Whatever they say next is going to change my life forever, good or bad, and I'm not sure I'm ready.

They pick my guitar up off of my lap and gently place it down on the floor. I sit on my hands to try and keep them from shaking as I wait for them to speak. The waiting is killing me. They lick their lips, and I hate how much it makes me want them. I shouldn't be allowed to want them after how awfully I treated them. I shouldn't be allowed to even consider it.

"Princess," they say after what feels like hours, their voice dripping with emotion. I pause for a moment at the nickname. That has to be a good sign, right? "You wrote that for me?"

"Yeah. I did," I whisper back. "I had a lot of help, but yeah, I wrote that just for you. I really fucked up. I know that. And I know I can't take back my actions, but if we can at least just be friends and get along for the sake of the band, I'd really like that. If you never want to talk to me again, I get that too and I will leave and you will never have to see me again. I'll quit the band if I have to. Whatever you want. I will do whatever you want." Tears are streaming down my cheeks now as I say those final words.

"Whatever I want you say..." They smirk with that teasing lilt in their voice that I've missed so much.

"Yeah. Whatever you want. Just tell me and I'll do it. Whatever I need to do to make this right."

"I think I have a pretty good idea of what you can do to make this right."

"You do?" I say, shock probably written all over my face. This was never meant to be this easy. They were meant to yell and scream at me and just be hurt and angry and all of the things.

"Kiss me," they say and I sputter for a second out of shock.

"You want me to kiss you? You don't want to yell at me and make me feel how you've felt for the past two weeks? You're just going to forgive me? Just like that?" There must be something seriously wrong here. There is no way that they're just willing to look past everything, and I doubt they really are, but did the song really just make it so easy? It shouldn't, right?

"Princess, just kiss me already." I can't contain myself anymore, I hold their face in my hands and kiss them like I've never kissed them before.

"So, I'm forgiven?" I ask as we finally pull away.

"I don't know…" They joke as they pretend to think about it. "Yes, princess, I probably shouldn't, but you came all the way out here looking like that and writing a song for me. It does things to me and how am I supposed to stay mad at you when you wrote me a song?"

"If I had known the way to your heart was through songs I would've written you songs years ago," I tease softly.

"Would you have? Years ago?"

"Baby, I've had a crush on you for just about as long as I've known you."

"And it took you how many years to act on it because?"

"Well, I didn't think you felt the same way about me, and then there was the whole thing with your relationship with Stevie, and don't even get me started on how long it took me to even figure out I'm gay."

"It took you that long, princess? Have you met yourself?"

"Haha, very funny. You were the first person I told when I figured it out," I say softly, looking down towards my hands in my lap, my nails painted a sparkly dark green, Finn's favorite color.

"I was the first person you told?"

"Yeah. And I was so scared to tell you. Which seems so stupid in hindsight. But I had just started figuring it out and didn't know what any of these feelings meant and you just always had it so together and seemed so sure of yourself and your sexuality and I didn't have anyone else I could really go to with it."

"Aren't, like, all of your friends some kind of gay?"

"That's one way to put it. But none of them were out at the time and we were all trying to figure it out, I guess. You were the only person who seemed to know one hundred percent who you were."

"Did I really come across like that? Was I that much of an asshole?"

"You weren't an asshole. You were sure of yourself in a way I could only dream to be. I think that's the first thing that made me attracted to you."

"Acting like a know-it-all?"

"No, dumbass, your confidence."

"Oh."

"Yeah."

"Why are you being so sappy all of a sudden?"

"I just really missed you. You were one of my best friends first, you know. I didn't just lose a partner when you stopped talking to me like that, I lost one of my best friends and one of my favorite people to be around." I start to tear up again and Finn reaches up to brush away a tear that rolls down my cheek.

"I'm one of your favorite people? Princess, that's just sad. You know so many cool people."

"Yet none of them make me laugh as hard as you do. Or make me feel as special as you do. You really do make me feel on top of the world. And I mean that in the corniest way possible. I've been falling in love with you since the day I met you and I actually don't know what I'd do if I were to lose you again."

"Well, princess, you won't ever have to worry about that because I've been falling in love with you since the day I met you, too. And one day we're going to get to live together in an apartment in this city and live the life we've always dreamed of."

"And that day might be coming sooner than you thought," I say with a big smile and a hint of excitement in my voice.

"Princess, don't mess with my emotions like that."

"I'm not messing with shit. I might have reached out to all the schools out here that accepted me and well, your school actually, the school that has always been my top choice, accepted me again. For the spring. So, we will have to do the whole long-distance thing for a few months, and I'm going to need to figure out housing because I can't get a spot in the dorms this late, but I'm making it happen."

"And what about your parents?"

"I might have exploded at my dad when I got home from tour and said everything I've been thinking for years. It wasn't a great choice, but it worked, and he realized how much he was actually hurting me and agreed to let me do what I actually want. And the funny thing is, it's not like I don't want to study business like he wants me to, but I want to specifically study music business so that I can just be better at all things band related. I think it also helped that I got recognized at the restaurant we went to and my dad really saw how big we're getting."

"You got recognized? Like in public?"

"It was really cool. I can't believe that's something that actually happens to us now."

"Yeah," they say wistfully. "I might have a solution for your living situation."

"Oh yeah?"

"Why don't you just move in with me? I do have an extra room here, if you want it, or you don't have to take it and could just move into my room." They look down towards their lap as they make the suggestion.

"I would love to move in with you. There's nothing I would want more. I'll talk to my parents, and we can work that out. But maybe we should head downstairs. Harper and Aspen are totally waiting to hear how this went. And so is Mari. We might have already sent the song to her and Stevie to get it on the album, if you're cool with that."

"I'm only cool with it if we get to keep your vocals on the song."

"I think we could make that work," I say with a smile as I grab their hand and we head down the stairs together.

Epilogue

Winter break was here before we knew it. Even with all of us in all different corners of the world, we still worked hard on our album to make it something that we were all proud of. We had a handful of really productive Zoom writing sessions, but we all mostly wrote songs on our own and brought them to the group during those sessions. Finn and Harper wrote most of the latter half of the album, being the best songwriters in the group, though I did contribute the song I wrote for Finn as well as many late night FaceTime writing sessions with Finn.

After those sessions, each of us, except Mari, took advantage of our school's recording equipment and worked hard to record our parts of the songs in a way that we were all happy with. It was simple enough, at least for most of us. Mari had some trouble depending on what country she was in at the time, but she made it work. And by made it work, I mean she didn't even have her bass with her so she really just approved whatever we all liked and as long as it sounded like something she could play, I would record it for her. It might not have been the most ideal situation, but she was doing so much traveling that taking an instrument with her wasn't really feasible. I guess I did understand that, and it did make sense for her, but even with her being somewhat absent from the conversations for the last few months, we'd been able to create an album that was sounding amazing.

And now, sitting around in Mari's garage, our favorite rehearsal space since graduating high school, we are going to be listening to our album all the way through, top to bottom, for the very first time. We decided on a late March release, and with a local show coming up, back at the restaurant we had played at all through high school, we thought there was no better time for us to announce the release of the album.

Even with us all in school and not actively touring or even creating new social media content with all of us being in our own little corners of the world, the band was still growing. Finn and I decided to start to be a bit more open about our relationship. We've decided to stop dodging the question. If someone asks us if we're together, we're not going to deny it, but if they don't ask then we don't really need to share that information. It's not all that important for us to deny it when it is so obvious. But at the same time, we don't need to be so public about it either.

I hold Finn on my lap as I pull the album up on my laptop and hit play on the fourteen-track masterpiece that we had created together. As the songs started playing, I look at my friends and bandmates, gauging their reactions to the masters that I had worked so hard on. We are announcing the album tonight and the release of our first single off of the album, Summer Sunsets, which we had been playing on tour already. Since playing it for the last few shows of the tour, demand for the song has been high and I'm so excited to finally get it out to our fanbase.

Watching everyone take in the album and enjoy the music we've made makes me feel as if I have finally done something right. Over the past few months, most of my free time has gone to working on the masters of each album track. I have worked so hard to create something that we could all be proud of.

When the last song finishes playing, the song I wrote for Finn, I close my laptop and look to my bandmates for their feelings, comments, reactions, and whatever they have to say.

"Princess, you did an amazing job with this. All that time you put into it has really paid off. It's great," Finn says, beaming up at me from their spot on my lap.

"We really did that, didn't we?" Harper says, pride evident in her eyes. "I want to listen to it again! We sound really good!" she says with a large smile spread across her cheeks.

"I think Kyle should just produce all of our albums from now until the end of time," Aspen says with an equally large smile. "Whatever you just did was magical. I still don't fully understand how you turned what we recorded into that masterpiece, but I'm so glad you did. It sounds amazing."

I look to Mari nervously, she has yet to say anything and for one of the most talkative members of the group, her silence can't be good. I raise an eyebrow at her, silently asking for her input. "I just don't know how to put how much I loved that into words. You are seriously talented, Kyle, what you just did on this album, it's amazing. Truly.

I can't wait to give this to all of our fans in just a few months."

I can't help but beam at the praise. Had I really created something that every single person in the room was loving? After a few minutes there's a knock on the door, and then Stevie walks in. I had sent her the masters a week prior to get her more professional opinion on them before finalizing them and bringing them to the group. After Finn and I worked everything out, the five of us had a really long conversation about if we wanted to move forward with Stevie as our manager since the tour was over and we could really go in any direction we wanted. We came to the decision that while she was not the best partner for Finn, she was a good fit for us as a band, at least for the time being, as long as we keep our relationship with her strictly professional.

"How are y'all feeling about tonight?" she asks as she looks around the room.

"More excited now that we've finally heard the album we're going to be announcing. Have you heard it yet? It's, like, really good!" Aspen says excitedly, speaking up before any of us have a chance, which was honestly surprising. She's normally so quiet.

"I have heard it. Kyle sent it to me a few weeks ago. It is really good. I'm glad you're all proud of it. I have the finalized cover to show you, if you're ready for that too," she says with a smile and receives lots of yeses and other excited noises.

She pulls out her own laptop and pulls up an image on her own device before turning it to face us. On her screen is a really cute picture of the five of us, sitting on and around a couch talking and laughing in our brightly colored outfits with all the colorful balloons and lots of glitter with the album title in big loopy letters: *Summer Sunsets.*

♫

We walk out onto the stage that we've played on all through high school to cheers louder than we have ever heard before. The stage was a smaller one than we had gotten used to performing on, but it felt like home.

We open with the same song we opened with on tour and fell right into that rhythm we had even though we haven't actually played together as a band for close to five months.

"Welcome back to what used to be our weekly show, we are The Undead Stars!" Harper says into her microphone to deafening cheers as we come to the end of the bridge of our very first song.

"Now I see a lot of familiar faces out in the crowd tonight, but it wouldn't hurt to introduce those of you who have never seen us before to my lovely bandmates," I say with a smile as the crowd roars. "On lead vocals we have our wonderful leading lady, and if you don't love her, you should, Harper!" More cheers. "Next to her on keys, we have the sweetest member of our group, Aspen!" There are more cheers and Mari raises a challenging eyebrow at me. "On bass we have the baddest bitch I know, Mari!" She smiles and nods approvingly as the crowd roars for her.

"And on drums we have my favorite person to be around, Finn!" Finn plays a little drum solo, and I can't help but turn and watch mesmerized.

"And we can't forget our incredibly sexy guitarist,

Kyle!" Finn yells into their microphone, and I feel myself blush ever so slightly. I haven't realized how much I have missed being on stage, but even more than that, I haven't realized how much I missed hearing Finn introducing me like that.

"And as Harper said we are The Undead Stars! We're going to have some fun tonight, if you'll let us!" The room fills with cheers as we begin to rev back up to get us to the final chorus of the song.

Our setlist for the show was the same as our tour setlist, and as we got to playing our unreleased, yet super popular song, Summer Sunsets, we began to gear up for the big announcement.

"So, if you were following our tour over the summer, you probably know what's coming next," I say hesitantly into my microphone to deafening screams from the front row of the crowd. I smile as I find Perri and Aubrey among the crowd with the biggest smiles on their faces, jumping with excitement as if they don't know what's coming next. "This has been the spot in the show where we play a certain unreleased song that I wrote for someone who is really special to me. Of course, I had help from the rest of my lovely bandmates because I am not that great when it comes to words, and we're going to get to that song in a minute."

The room is filled with excited cheers and the girls at the very front, the few fans that we had noticed following us from show to show, scream with such an excitement I can't keep it in any longer. "And if it wasn't obvious by our love for playing the song, it is going to be the first single off of our new album which shares the same title. Summer Sunsets, the album, will be out on all streaming platforms March twenty-first next year, so mark your calendars and get ready." The cheers are unlike anything we had heard before, and I stand back looking between my friends and the fans trying to gauge how big this was going to be for us.

"And the song that we're about to play, the title track of our album, will be out on all streaming platforms in just three weeks on January tenth!" Mari calls into her microphone to more cheers from the fans.

We play Summer Sunsets and for the first time there are people in the room singing the words right back to us. With the other songs we had performed, the songs from our self-titled EP and the songs that we've covered during the tour, I was able to get used to the fans or just people in the audience singing the songs back at us, but here in this space, performing a song that has yet to be released, and seeing fans singing along and knowing all the words warmed something in my heart in a way I didn't quite know how to explain.

We come off the stage after the show and a mix of emotions runs through me. It is bittersweet in a way, the little restaurant that we played in had been our home all through high school and to be able to come back and perform a show that filled the space to the point that people were getting turned away was just a full circle moment.

"I don't think I realized how much I missed playing with y'all," Mari says with a teary smile as we pack up our instruments and other things in the small backstage area. "And I don't think I realized how much I missed playing here."

"It's weird, I thought playing up there was going to

feel so weird after playing in bigger venues on bigger stages, but it just felt like home," Aspen says, and when I look over at her I see her tearing up too.

Someone walks in the backstage area and, before any of us could say anything, she saunters right over to Mari and places a quick kiss on her lips.

"Looks like Europe's been good to you," I say to Mari with a smile. "I didn't realize you brought someone home with you."

"The program's got some pretty cool people. I think I got pretty lucky to find such a cool group of friends there," Mari smiles. "But we're going to be late for dinner with my parents if we don't head out," Mari grabs the girl's hand. "Check your phones later. I'll fill you in then I promise." She turns and heads out the back door that we'd been using since high school.

"Anyone want to grab food or do y'all have to get home too?" I ask the rest of the group, not yet ready to go home.

"I promised my parents I'd be home for dinner after our show, sorry," Harper says with a sad little smile, "but we'll catch up before we all have to go back to school."

I smile and nod as Aspen mumbles something along the same lines and follows Harper out, leaving just Finn and me in the room.

"Are your parents expecting you home anytime soon or do you want to head into town for a little date night? I know it's only been a week since we last saw each other, but I've missed you so much baby."

Finn looks at their phone and then back to me with a huge smile spread across their face. "My parents aren't expecting me home for another two hours. I'm free to go wherever you want, princess."

I smoothly make my way through the airport, checking my bags and getting through security. I'm sitting at the gate with about ten minutes until boarding when Finn calls.

"Hi baby," I say softly, trying not to disturb anyone else in the airport.

"You're at the airport already?" they ask and I can hear the smile in their voice.

"Yeah. Only a few more hours until I'm back with you. I'm still mad you had to go back early and left me here all on my own for three whole weeks," I say, hoping they can hear my pout in my voice.

"I know princess, but I couldn't pass up the opportunity for research with my professor already. Do you know how many freshmen get an offer like this?"

"I know, baby. And I'm so proud of you. I just assumed we'd be flying out together."

"I know princess, maybe next time. I can't wait for you to get here and get all moved in."

"Me too. I can't wait to start school with you. The school out here was fun and all, but you know you're where I've always wanted to be."

"I know princess, and you're so close. So, so close"

"Just seven hours and we'll be back in the same city."

"And I'll be picking you up from the airport and driving you to our apartment."

"I still can't believe we get to call it *our* apartment."

"Well, get used to it princess. It's your home now too."

"I know. It just doesn't feel real."

"To you. I've been getting your fifteen million amazon packages and having to carry each and every one up the stairs."

"I'm sorry, that sounds like a lot."

"It has been a lot, but I wouldn't trade it for anything. I can't wait to get you in my arms so soon."

The boarding call for my flight blares over the speakers and we say our goodbyes and hang up with just enough time for me to join the line and board my flight.

Just like the last flight I had been on, one in the opposite direction, I decided to spend the time working on the deluxe tracks for album, which we haven't even announced yet. Though this time I have a harder time focusing on the music. I find myself listening to the same parts over and over and then forgetting what I was trying to do.

Finn had sounded so excited over the phone and I just know that when I land in LA, and we finally get to be together again, we're going to be unstoppable. School is just going to be a stop on our rise to mega stardom and with the album release just months away, we're really on our way there.

By the time the flight lands, I've barely gotten any work done, not that I had much to do other than a few readings for the classes I'll be starting in a few weeks. But I couldn't be too mad at my lack of productivity though. My mind was clearly elsewhere.

I walk off the plane and through the maze that is the airport until I get to baggage claim and, as I'm walking there, I finally see Finn and can't help but break out into a jog as I rush to get them in my arms.

"Hi baby," I say in a soft whisper as I gently set my bags down and wrap my arms around their waist. "I missed you so much."

"I missed you too, princess," they say in between sniffles into the crook of my neck.

"I've come to solve all of your problems," I joke with a smile as they pull away. "And build all of your furniture."

"You mean all the furniture you ordered on amazon and made me carry up the stairs?"

I can't help but laugh as they pout ever so slightly. "Yeah. That furniture."

"Good. The boxes seem to want to overtake the whole apartment."

"Good thing I'm here to fix that, then." I smile as we stand at the carousel and wait for my bags.

"How the hell did you travel with so much shit?" they tease.

"I'm moving. I need a lot of stuff."

"Princess, I didn't ask why. I asked how. Two completely different questions."

"Like this," I say as I hold two suitcases in each hand and wheel them out, following Finn towards their car.

"You're ridiculous."

"You love me."

"Unfortunately, I do."

"Unfortunately?" I act shocked and then pull them in for a chaste kiss, reveling in the fact that I get to have them in my arms again. They giggle and we load my suitcases into the trunk of their car.

The drive to their—*our*—apartment is familiar, and it

just feels so amazing looking out at the city and knowing that this is now my home. Everything I've ever wanted was to live here and now I'm finally getting to live out that dream and I can't be more excited.

Finn snatches up one of my suitcases and drags me into the apartment the second we arrive. Once the door is firmly closed, and locked, they push me up against it and lean up to kiss me. I let my other bags fall to the floor as I hold them close to me and return their embrace. It's only been a few weeks since we were last together, but even still I'd missed them so much.

After a while, I drag Finn into the barely unpacked living room and kitchen and look around the space. My new home now. Boxes are strewn everywhere, all addressed to me, and I know the mess is fully my fault, but I can't wait to get to unpacking it together.

"You've made some good progress on unpacking my boxes, baby, I'm proud of you," I say as I eye the handful of empty boxes in the corner and see some of the décor items I ordered littered around the space.

"We're going to have to make a pretty big target run," they say nervously. "We only have a few pots and pans, and no plates or utensils. I've been using the plastic ones. The kid who was in your room semester took all of their stuff back, and I wanted to pick them out with you."

"We can do that. We're also going to have to figure out what we want to do with the other bedroom."

"You mean your room?"

"After this summer you're going to make me sleep in the other room?" I jokingly place my hand on my heart and try to look offended. "I thought we'd share a room.

Maybe I'll use the closet space for my clothes, but I thought the room was ours to share."

"Did you now, princess? I don't know, I really like having my own space in the bed. It's been nice not sharing a bed."

"Oh really? You always seem to love my personal space in our bed too." I smirk as they start to blush.

"Well, I can't help but want to be all over you, can I princess?" I can't help but smile and give them another small kiss.

"I was thinking, and maybe this is a bad idea, but we could turn that room into a little makeshift studio type room? We're going to need to buy some more equipment anyways since we're going to start working on the next album, and we do have such a nice space we could use for working on it. We could even do a little reorganizing and maybe move your desk into there and treat it like an office."

"Sounds like we've got a lot of work to do today," Finn says, wrapping their arms around my neck yet again.

"Maybe the work can wait," I say after a few moments, breaking the peaceful silence. "I've already had such a long day. I know it's only the early afternoon here, but it's dinner time back home."

"You're not actually saying you got jet lagged over a single day, are you?"

"I'm not, not saying that." I chuckled.

"Your body must be all sorts of out of whack," they tease.

"It really is. But maybe you could help me get it back to the proper time zone."

"I think all you're going to need is a really good night's sleep."

"You think that's it, baby? Just some good sleep?" I ask raising an eyebrow.

"Yeah, just some really good sleep. In my bed," they add playfully.

"Oh, it's *your* bed?" I smirk and raise an eyebrow.

"What did you think it was?" they giggle.

"I guess I was thinking it was our bed." I grin playfully, knowing I am probably right.

"Well, the last time I checked, the room was mine, not ours, but now that you're here…" Their voice trails off as they grab my hand dragging me into the bedroom. "I guess this could be our room now. If you think you deserve that."

"Of course, I think I deserve that. I just moved across the country for you."

"Just for me?"

"That might be a slight exaggeration, but you are a big part of it." I smile as I sit down on the bed, pulling them into my lap. "But I wouldn't have finally stood up for myself against everything my dad was saying if it wasn't for you and only you."

"Only me?" they ask.

"Yeah, baby, only you." I grab their face in my hands and pull them in for a deep and passionate kiss. We can worry about unpacking later.

Acknowledgments

This book would not have been possible without the amazing people in my life who have guided me to this moment.

To my amazing parents for supporting my dreams and aspirations no matter how crazy they may have seemed.

To my brother Zach for always sticking by my side.

To Kimberly for spending hours with me while I talked through my struggles with this book as I started writing it.

To Madison for our countless late nights writing with a bottle of wine. I don't know how I would have gotten through the first draft without you.

To Nina. You stuck by my side through every single step of the process. From study dates on the weekends to late nights in the library, countless cups of coffee, and hours spent crying in your car. I wouldn't have been able to get this book done without your love and support and I'm so lucky to call you one of my best friends.

To Falyn. You've seen this book every single step of the way. This story wouldn't be what it is without our many FaceTime calls at all hours of the day and night. Your unwavering support has meant more than you will ever know. This story is ours.

To all of my lovely teachers. Your support has always had a deep impact on me.

To Jade, my amazing editor for guiding me and shaping this book into something I am truly proud of.

And lastly, to every single person who has loved me and supported me through the many stages and phases of my life. To you all I am incredibly grateful.

About the Author

Jacqueline Elisabeth is a twenty-three-year-old author from New Jersey. She recently graduated from Skidmore College majoring in Sociology with a double minor in English and Arts Administration. Her love for storytelling has led her to writing authentic stories about what falling in love looks like for queer and Jewish young adults.

https://jacqueline-elisabeth.wixsite.com/website

instagram.com/writerjelisabeth

tiktok.com/@writerjelisabeth

youtube.com/@AuthorJacquelineElisabeth

Also by Jacqueline Elisabeth

The Eight Slopes of Chanukah

www.ingramcontent.com/pod-product-compliance
Lightning Source LLC
Chambersburg PA
CBHW022122310726
48972CB00007B/2146